MARTYN PIG

MART

UP

YN PIG

A NOVEL BY KEVIN BROOKS

SCHOLASTIC INC.

New York Toronto London Auckland Sydney
Mexico City New Delhi Hong Kong Buenos Aires.

ISBN 0-439-44085-8

Text copyright © 2002 by Kevin Brooks. All rights reserved.
Published by Scholastic Inc., 557 Broadway, New York, NY 10012,
by arrangement with The Chicken House. THE CHICKEN HOUSE
and associated logos are trademarks of The Chicken House.
SCHOLASTIC and associated logos are trademarks
and/or registered trademarks of Scholastic Inc.

12 11 10 9 8 7 6 5 4 3 2 1   2 3 4 5 6 7/0

Printed in the U.S.A.   0 1

First Scholastic paperback printing, October 2002

CONTENTS

MARTYN PIG

WEDNESDAY

It's hard to know where to start with this. I suppose I could tell you all about where I was born, what it was like when Mom was still around, what happened when I was a little kid, all that kind of stuff, but it's not really relevant. Or maybe it is. I don't know. Most of it I can't remember, anyway. It's all just bits and pieces of things, things that may or may not have happened — scraps of images, vague feelings, faded photographs of nameless people and forgotten places — that kind of thing.

Anyway, let's get the name out of the way first.

Martyn Pig.

Martyn with a Y, Pig with an I and one G.

Martyn Pig.

Yeah, I know. Don't worry about it. It doesn't bother me anymore. I'm used to it. But, there was a time when nothing else seemed to matter. My name made my life unbearable. Martyn Pig. Why? Why did I have to put up with it? The startled looks, the sneers and sniggers, the snorts, the never-ending pig jokes, day in, day out, over and over again. Why? Why me? Why couldn't I have a *normal* name? Keith Watson, Darren Jones — something like that. Why was I lumbered with a name that turned heads, a name that got me noticed? A *funny* name. Why?

And it wasn't just the name-calling I had to worry about, either, it was everything. Every time I had to tell someone my name I'd start to feel ill. Physically ill. Sweaty hands, the shakes, bellyache. I lived for years with the constant dread of having to announce myself.

"Name?"

"Martyn Pig."

"Pardon?"

"Martyn Pig."

"Pig?"

"Yes."

"Martyn Pig?"

"Yes. Martyn with a Y, Pig with an I and one G."

Unless you've got an odd name yourself you wouldn't know what it's like. You wouldn't understand. They say that sticks and stones may break your bones but words will never hurt you. Oh, yeah? Well, whoever thought that one up was an idiot. An idiot with an ordinary name, probably. Words *hurt*. Porky, Piggy, Pigman, Oink, Bacon, Stinky, Snorter, Porker, Grunt . . .

I blamed my dad. It was his name. I asked him once if he'd ever thought of changing it.

"Changing what?" he'd muttered, without looking up from his newspaper.

"Our name. Pig."

He reached for his beer and said nothing.

"Dad?"

"What?"

"Nothing. It doesn't matter."

It took me a long time to realize that the best way to deal with name-calling is to simply ignore it. It's not easy, but I've found that if you let people do or think what they want and don't let your feelings get too mixed up in it, then after a while they usually get bored and leave you alone.

It worked for me, anyway. I still have to put up with curious looks whenever I give my name. New teachers, librarians, doctors, dentists, newsagents, they all do it: narrow their eyes, frown, look to one side — is he joking? And then the embarrassment when they realize I'm not. But I can cope with that. Like I said, I'm used to it. You can get used to just about anything given enough time.

At least I don't get called Porky anymore. Well . . . not very often.

This — what I'm going to tell you about — it all happened just more than a year ago. It was the week before Christmas. Or Xmas, as Dad called it. Exmas. It was the week before Exmas. A Wednesday.

I was in the kitchen filling a plastic garbage bag with empty beer bottles and Dad was leaning in the doorway, smoking a cigarette, watching me through bloodshot eyes.

"Don't you go takin' 'em to the recycling center," he said.

"No, Dad."

"Dreadful emviroment this, emviroment that . . . if anyone wants to use my empty bottles again they'll have to pay for 'em. I don't get 'em for nothing, you know."

"No."

"Why should I give 'em away? What's the emviroment ever done for me?"

"Mmm."

"Bloody recycling centers . . ."

He paused to puff on his cigarette. I thought of telling him that there's no such thing as the *emviroment*, but I couldn't be bothered. I filled the garbage bag, tied it, and started on another. Dad was gazing at his reflection in the glass door, rubbing at the bags under his eyes. He could have been quite a handsome man if it wasn't for the drink. Handsome in a short, thuggish kind of way. Five foot seven, tough-guy mouth, squarish jaw, oily black hair. He could have looked like one of those bad guys in films — the ones the ladies can't help falling in love with, even though they know they're bad — but he didn't. He looked like what he was: a drunk. Fat little belly, florid skin, yellowed eyes, sagging cheeks, and a big fat neck. Old and worn-out at forty.

He leaned over the sink, coughed, spat, and flicked ash down the drain. "That bloody woman's coming Friday."

"That bloody woman" was my Aunty Jean. Dad's older sister. A terrible woman. Think of the worst person you know, then double it, and you'll be halfway to Aunty Jean. I can hardly bear to describe her, to tell you the truth. Furious is the first word that comes to mind. Mad, ugly, and furious. An angular woman, cold and hard, with wiry blue hair and a face that makes you shudder. I don't know what color her eyes are, but they look as if they never close. They have about as much warmth as two depthless pools. Her mouth is thin and fire-engine red, like something drawn by a disturbed child. And she walks faster than most people run. She moves like a huntress, quick and quiet, honing in on her prey. When I was younger I had nightmares about her. I still do.

She always came over the week before Christmas. I don't know what for. All she ever did was sit around moaning about everything for about three hours. And when she wasn't moaning about everything she was swishing around the house running her fingers through the dust, checking in the cupboards, frowning at the state of the windows, tutting at everything.

"My *God*, William, how can you *live* like this."

Everyone else called my dad Billy, but Aunty Jean always called him by his full name, pronouncing it with an over-emphasis on the first syllable — *Will*-yam — that made him flinch whenever she said it. He detested her. Hated her. He was scared stiff of the woman. What he'd do, he'd hide all his bottles before she came over. Up in the attic, mostly. It took him ages. Up and down the ladder, arms full of clinking bottles, his face getting redder and redder by the minute, muttering under his breath all the time, "Bloody woman, bloody woman, bloody woman, bloody woman . . ."

Normally he didn't care what anyone thought about his drinking, but with Aunty Jean it was different. You see, when Mom left us — this was years ago — Aunty Jean tried to get custody of me. She wanted me to live with her, not with Dad. God knows why, she never liked me. But then she liked Dad even less, blamed him for the divorce and everything, said that he'd driven Mom to the "brink of despair" and that she wasn't going to "stand by and let him ruin an innocent young boy's life, too." Which was all a load of garbage. She didn't give a hoot for my innocent life, she just wanted to kick Dad while he was down, kick him where it hurts, leave him with nothing. She despised him as much as he despised her. I don't know why. Some kind of brother/sister thing, I suppose. Anyway, her plan was to expose Dad as a drunkard. She reckoned the authorities would decide in her favor once they knew of Dad's wicked, drunken ways. They'd never allow me to live with a boozer. But she underestimated Dad. His need for me was greater than hers. Without me, he was just a drunk. But with me, he was a drunk with responsibilities, a drunk with welfare benefits, a drunk with someone to clean up the puke.

After he was given notice that Aunty Jean had applied for custody he didn't so much as look at a bottle for two months or more. Not a drop. Not a sniff. It was remarkable. He shaved, washed, wore a suit, he even smiled now and then. I almost grew to like him. Aunty Jean's custody case was dead in the water. She didn't stand a chance. As far as the rest of the world was concerned, Mr. William Pig was the *ideal father*.

The day I was officially assigned to Dad's loving care, he went out drinking and didn't come back for three days. When he did come back — unshaven, red-eyed, stinking — he slouched into the kitchen where I was making some tea, leaned down at me, grinning like a madman, and slurred right into my face: "Remember me?"

Then he stumbled over to the sink and threw up.

So that's why he hid the bottles. He didn't want to give Aunty Jean any excuse for reopening the custody debate. It wasn't so much the thought of losing me that worried him, it was the thought of staying sober for another two months.

• • •

"Dreadful woman," he muttered again as I started on the empty beer cans, stamping them down into flattened disks, filling up another garbage bag. "She's coming at four," he went on, "day after tomorrow, so make sure the place is cleaned up."

"Yeah," I said, wiping stale beer from the palms of my hands and reaching for another blue bag. Dad watched for a while longer, then turned and slouched off into the front room.

Christmas meant nothing to us. It was just a couple of weeks off school for me and a good excuse for Dad to drink, not that he ever needed one. There was no festive spirit, no goodwill to all men, no wreaths, no holly — just cold, rainy days with nothing much to do.

I spent most of that Wednesday afternoon in town. Dad had given me some money — two dirty twenties — and told me to "get some stuff in for Exmas: turkey, potatoes, presents . . . carrots, stuff like that." It was too early to get the food in, Christmas was still a week away, but I wasn't going to argue. If he wanted me to go shopping, I'd go shopping. It gave me something to do.

Halfway down the street I heard a shout — *"Mar'n!"* — and turned to see Dad leaning out of the bedroom window, bare-chested, a cigarette dangling from his lip.

"Don't forget the bloody whasnames," he yelled, making a yanking movement with both hands, tugging on two invisible ropes.

"What?" I called back.

He took the cigarette from his mouth, gazed blankly into the distance for a moment, then blurted out, "Cookies! Get some bloody Exmas cookies. Big ones, mind, not them tiny ones."

● ● ●

In town, outside Sainsbury's, the scariest Santa Claus I'd ever seen was slumped in the back of a plywood sleigh. He was thin and short. So thin that his big black Santa's belt wound twice around his waist. Stiff black stubble showed on his chin beneath an ill-fitting, off-white Santa beard and — strangest of all, I thought — a pair of brand-new sneakers gleamed on his feet. When he *Ho-ho-ho*'ed he sounded like a serial killer. Six plywood reindeer pulled his plywood sleigh. They were painted a shiny chocolate brown, with glittery red eyes and coat-hanger antlers entwined with plastic holly.

It was raining.

I watched the skinny Santa for a while — thirty seconds and a Lucky Bag per kid — then headed off toward the other end of town. As I walked I got to thinking about the whole Santa Claus thing. I was trying to remember if I'd ever really believed that a fat man in a fat red suit could squeeze down a million different chimneys all in one night. I suppose I must have believed it at some point. I have a very vague memory of sitting on a Santa's knee when I was about three or four years old. I can still remember the nasty, scratchy feel of his red nylon trousers, the stickiness of his beard, and a strange fruity smell. When I asked him where he lived a familiar slurred voice answered, "Poland . . . uh . . . North Poland . . . in an underground igloo with twenty-two dwarves — *hic* — and a reindeer."

It was still raining when I got to the Bargain Bin. It's one of those cheap stores that sell all kinds of junk — cups, towels, bean bags, pencil cases. Upstairs, there's a toy department full of footballs and plastic machine guns that make noises. You can test them. There's an arrow pointing to the trigger that says Press and when you pull the trigger they go *kakakakakakaka* or *dugga-dugga-dugga-dugga-peow-peow*. Ricochets. I was just looking around, looking at the racks of little toys — plastic animals, cows, sheep, crocodiles, rubber snakes, water pistols. I thought I might find something there for Alex, a present. Nothing serious, just a little something, you know, a token. The year before I'd bought her a box of plastic ants. I don't remember what she gave me.

Anyway, I was just standing there staring at the toys on the wall, trying to find something I thought she'd like, something I could afford, when I suddenly realized that I wasn't really looking at anything at all. I was looking, but not seeing. It was the noise. I couldn't concentrate because of the noise. Horrible tinny Christmas Muzak blaring out from speakers in the ceiling, synthesized sleigh bells and chirpy pianos, groany old singers trying too hard to be happy — it was unbearable. A great swirling mess of sound searing its way into my head. I tried to ignore it, but it just seemed to get louder and louder. And it was too hot in there, too. It was boiling. There was no air. I couldn't breathe. The sound was paralyzing — chattering machine guns, talking animals, wailing police car sirens, *dee-dur dee-dur dee-dur*, parents shouting at their kids, whacking them on the arm, the kids screaming and crying, the constant *beep beep beep* of the registers, the music . . . it was like something out of a nightmare.

I had to get out.

I went and sat in the square for a while. The rain had stopped but the air was moist and cold. The sweat running down my neck felt clammy and foreign. I sat on a low brick wall and watched limping pigeons peck at food scabs while the slurred whine of a beardy old street performer drifted across from the nearby shopping arcade. He's always there, always playing the same depressing song. *When I'm old with only one eye, I'll do nothing but look at the sky. . . .* Two screaming children clutching bits of bread were chasing pigeons across the square, and in the background I could hear the constant sound of thousands of people shuffling around the crowded streets, all talking, jabbering away, yammering rubbish to each other — *scuffle scuffle scuffle, blah blah blah, scuffle scuffle scuffle*. From distant streets the discordant sounds of other street performers mingled awkwardly with the hubbub — a hurdy-gurdy, the *plink-plonk* of a banjo, Peruvian pipes, the screaming whistle of a flute. . . .

It all sounded like madness to me. Too many people, too many buildings, too much noise, too much everything.

It's there all the time, the sound of too much everything, but no one ever listens to it. Because once you start to listen, you can never stop, and in the end it'll drive you crazy.

A wild-haired loony munching a greasy burger sat down next to me and grinned in my direction. Bits of food clung to his teeth. I decided to move on. I was cold and wet from sitting on the damp wall and it was starting to rain again. I walked up through the backstreets then cut down through the multistory garage, across the road bridge, then down past the library to the street market where shifty-looking men in long nylon overcoats and fingerless gloves were standing at their stalls drinking steaming coffee from styrofoam cups. More noise — crappy rock 'n' roll music, loud Christmas carols, marketmen shouting out above the clamor: *Getchur luvverly turkeys 'ere! . . . Plenny*

a luvverly turkeys! . . . Wrappin' papah! Five sheets a buck! . . .
Getchur luvverly wrappin' papah 'ere!

I bought the first turkey I came across. A wet-looking white thing in a bag. In a week's time it would probably taste even worse than it looked, but it didn't matter. Dad would be so drunk on Christmas Day he'd eat anything. He'd eat a seagull if I dished one up. Raw.

I got carrots and potatoes, a fruitcake, chips, a box of cheap cookies and a bargain pack of Christmas decorations. Then I lugged it all home.

It was dark when I got back. My arms ached from carrying the shopping, my hands and feet were frozen, and I had a stiff neck. And I was getting a cold. Snot dripped from the end of my nose and I had to keep stopping to put down the shopping bags so I could wipe it.

Alex was waiting at the bus stop. She waved and I crossed over.

"Your nose is running," she said.

"Yeah, I know," I said, wiping it on my sleeve. "Where're you going?"

"Dean's."

"Oh."

"What's in the bags?" she asked.

"Christmas stuff."

"Anything for me?"

"Maybe."

"More ants?" She grinned.

"You never know."

When she smiled I'd sometimes get this sick feeling in my

stomach, like . . . I don't know what it was like. One of those feelings when you don't know if it's good or if it's bad. One of those.

I rested the shopping bags on the ground and watched cars droning up and down the road. Metal, rubber, fumes, people, all moving from place to place, going somewhere, doing something. The inside of the concrete bus shelter was depressingly familiar: a glassless timetable poster, torn and defaced, bits of wet muck all over the place, mindless scribbles on the walls — *Dec + Lee . . . YEAAH MAN! . . . Duffy is hot. . . .* I sat down on the folding seat beside Alex.

"Fed up?" she asked.

"I'm all right."

She leaned over and peered into the shopping bags, nudging one with a foot. "Nice-looking chicken," she said, smiling.

"It's a turkey," I said.

"Bit *small* for a turkey."

"It's a small turkey."

"I think you'll find that's a chicken, Martyn."

She grinned at me and I grinned back. Her eyes shone like marbles, clear and round and perfect.

"Did you see the Elvises?" she asked.

"What?"

"In town, at the precinct. There was a load of people all dressed up as Elvis Presley. You know, with the big sunglasses and sideburns, funny white suits with great big collars? Didn't you see them?"

"No."

"There were all sorts — fat ones, thin ones. . . ."

"Why were they dressed up as Elvis Presley?"

"I don't know. For Christmas, I suppose."

"What's Elvis Presley got to do with Christmas?"

"They were singing carols."

I looked at her. "A *choir* of Elvises?"

She shook her head, laughing. "It's for charity."

"Oh *well*, that's all right then."

She looked away and waved at a girl across the street. I didn't know who it was, just a girl. I rubbed the back of my neck. I was still sweating, but not so bad anymore. The bus shelter stank. My sleeve was caked with frozen snot and my feet were getting more numb by the second. But despite all that, I felt OK. Just sitting there, chatting, doing nothing, watching the world go by —

"Here's the bus," Alex said, digging in her bag for her purse. "I've got to go. I'll see you later."

"OK."

The bus pulled in, the doors *pished* open, and Alex stepped on. "About ten?" she called out over her shoulder.

"OK."

I watched her pay. I watched the bus driver click buttons on his ticket machine and I watched the bus ticket snicker out. I watched the way her eyes blinked slowly and I watched her mouth say *Thank you* and I watched the coal-black shine of her hair as she took the bus ticket and rolled it into a tube and stuck it in the corner of her mouth. I watched her hitch up the collar of her army jacket and I saw the bright white flash of her T-shirt beneath the open folds of her jacket as she strolled gracefully to the back of the bus. And I watched and waited in vain for her to turn her head as the bus lurched out into the street, shuddered up the road, and disappeared around the corner.

She never looked back.

I first met Alex about two years ago when she and her mom moved into a rented house just down the road from us. I remember watching from my bedroom window as they unloaded all their stuff from a moving van, and I remember thinking to myself how nice she looked. Nice. She looked nice. Pretty. Kind of scruffy, with straggly black hair sticking out from a shapeless black hat. She wore battered old jeans and a long red sweater. I liked the way she walked, too. An easy lope.

What if . . . I'd thought to myself. What if I went over and said hello? Hello, I'm Martyn, welcome to the street. Something like that. I could do that, couldn't I? It wouldn't be too hard. Hi! My name's Martyn, how's it going. . . .

Don't be ridiculous. Not in a million years.

She was fifteen then, and I was fourteen. Nearly fourteen, anyway. All right, I was thirteen. She was a young woman, I was just a gawky-looking kid.

It was a ridiculous idea.

So I just watched from the window. I watched her as she climbed up into the back of the van. I watched her as she lugged the stuff out and passed it to her mom. I watched her jump down from the van and slap the dust from her jeans. I watched her as she bounced up the path carrying a big green vase in both hands, and I watched as she stumbled over a loose paving stone and the vase went flying into the air and landed on the doorstep with a big hollow smash. Now she's going to get it, I thought.

But when her mom came out they just stared at each other for a second, looked down at the shards of green glass strewn all over the place, and then started laughing. Just stood there giggling and hooting like a couple of crazy people. I couldn't believe it. If that was me, Dad would have screamed his head off and thumped me on the back of the head.

When they eventually stopped laughing Alex's mom started clearing up the broken glass, carefully picking up the big bits and putting them into a box. She was quite tall, for a woman. Sort of dumpy, too. Medium-tall and dumpy, if that makes any sense. Her hair was black, like Alex's, but short. And her face was sort of gray and tired-looking, like her skin needed watering. She wore faded jeans and a black T-shirt, long beady earrings, and bracelets on her wrists. As she hefted the box of broken glass and turned to go back into the house she glanced up in my direction. I looked away. When she came back out, carrying a dustpan and brush, she sneaked another look up at my window, then stooped down and started to sweep up the rest of the broken vase. She must have said something because, just as I was about to disappear from the window, Alex turned and flashed a big grin at me and waved.

"Hey!"

I gave an embarrassed half-wave.

"Are you busy?" she shouted.

"What?"

"Are you busy?" she repeated. "Come and give us a hand if you're not."

I nodded yes and immediately regretted it. Dumb thing to do. Forget it.

I quickly changed into a clean T-shirt then tiptoed down the stairs so as not to wake Dad, who was sleeping off his lunch in the front room, and went out into the street. Walking across the road toward the moving van my legs felt like rubber bands. I'd forgotten how to walk. I was a wobbling fool.

Alex smiled at me and my legs almost gave up.

"Hello," she said.

"Hello."

"Alexandra Freeman," she said, "Alex."

"Martyn," I said, nodding my head up and down like an imbecile. "Uh . . . Martyn."

"This is my mom."

"Hello, Martyn," her mom said. "Pleased to meet you."

"Ditto," I said.

Alex giggled.

It felt all right.

Now, after Alex had left on the bus, I trudged across the road feeling even worse than I'd felt before. The OK feeling from the bus shelter had evaporated. Bummed. That's how I felt. I felt bummed. Bummed as a . . . whatever. Something bummed. I always felt bad when she was seeing Dean. Dean was her boyfriend. Dean West. He was eighteen, he worked in the Gadget Shop in town — computers, sound systems, electronic stuff. He was an idiot. Ponytail, long fingernails, bad skin. His face was all the same color — lips, cheeks, eyes, nose — all rotten and white. He rode a motorcycle and liked to think he was some kind of biker, but he wasn't. He was just a pale white idiot.

I bumped into them once in town, Alex and Dean. In CVS.

I was waiting for Dad's prescription when I spotted them over by the photo booth. Dean in his usual black biker gear, pale face ugly and even whiter than usual beneath the cold shop lights, flicking his ponytail from side to side like a cow flicking at flies with its tail. Alex wore a leather jacket, too, which I'd never seen before. She looked good in it. She also looked a bit bored. When she smiled at Dean I could tell she didn't really mean it. I liked that. They were waiting for their photos to come out. Dumb, jokey photos, no doubt. Funny faces, ha ha ha. I turned away, pretending to study packets of medicine in the pharmacy counter, hoping Dad's prescription would hurry up so I could leave.

"Martyn!" It was Alex's voice.

I turned and said hello with mock surprise. Dean had his arm around Alex's shoulder.

"This is Dean," Alex said.

I nodded.

"Well," he drawled, looking me up and down, "the Pigman. At last we meet. I've heard all about you."

I didn't know what to say, so I said nothing.

"Got the shits, have you?" he said.

"What?"

He nodded his head at the pharmacy counter. I looked at the packets I'd been studying: diarrhea remedies.

I tried a smile. "No . . . no, a prescription. I'm waiting for my dad's prescription."

"Yeah," sneered Dean.

I looked at Alex, hoping for support. She looked away, embarrassed.

"Come on," Dean said to Alex, pulling on her shoulder.

I'm sure she stiffened slightly at his touch, but they moved off, anyway.

"See you, Martyn," Alex called over her shoulder.

Dean, idiotically, winked at me.

It wasn't that I was jealous. Well, I suppose I was a bit jealous. But not in a wimpy kind of way, you know, not in a snotty, pouty kind of way. No, that wasn't it. Not really. That wasn't the reason I was bummed. All right, it was *partly* the reason. But the main thing was — it was just *wrong*. All of it. Alex and Dean. Wrong. It stank. It was wrong for her to spend time with him. It was a waste. He was nothing. It was wrong. Wrong. Wrong. *Wrong*. She was too good for him.

The rain was turning to sleet as I pushed open the back gate and shuffled down the alleyway that led to the back of our house, stepping over dog turds and squashed cigarette ends and trash bags full of empty beer cans.

What's it got to do with you, anyway? I was thinking to myself. She can see who she wants. *What's it got to do with you? What it's got to do with me?*

What?

I paused for a moment, wondering just who the hell I was arguing with, then shrugged and went in through the kitchen door.

"About bloody time, too."

Dad was standing at the back window in his multi-stained vest, swigging beer and smoking a cigarette and spraying shaving foam onto the kitchen window. I looked at him, said nothing, and put the shopping bags on the top of the fridge.

"Change?" he said, holding out his hand. I gave him whatever was left of the money. He sniffed at it, then put it in his pocket and went over to the shopping. "Did you get it all?"

"I think so."

"You'd better more than jus' think so," he said, dipping into one of the bags.

I didn't have a clue what he meant. Neither did he, I expect. He grunted through a shopping bag, poking this and poking that, cigarette ash dropping all over the place, then he stopped and looked up at me and said, "Where're the cookies?"

"In the other bag," I told him.

"Oh, right." He shrugged and turned to the window. "What do you think?"

Creamy-white shaving foam dripped all over the window, great globs of it sliding down the glass and piling up on the windowsill in little soapy mountains. At first I thought it was some kind of half-assed attempt at cleaning, but that didn't make sense because Dad *never* did any cleaning . . . and then I got it. It was supposed to be snow. Christmas decorations.

"Very nice, Dad," I said. "Good idea."

"Yeah, well . . ." he said, losing interest. "Best get that stuff put away before it rots."

Did I hate him? He was a drunken slob and he treated me like dirt. What do *you* think? Of course I hated him. You would have hated him, too, if you'd ever met him. God knows why Mom ever married him. Probably for the same reason that Alex went out with Dean. Some kind of mental short circuit somewhere. Yeah, I hated him. I hated every inch of him. From his broken-veined, red-nosed face to his dirty, stinking feet. I hated his beery guts.

But I never meant to kill him.

Things don't just happen, they have reasons. And the reasons have reasons. And the reasons for the reasons have reasons. And then the things that happen make other things happen, so they become reasons themselves. Nothing moves forward in a straight line, nothing is straightforward. Which is why, in a funny kind of way, it was *The Complete Illustrated Sherlock Holmes* that killed my dad. If I hadn't got *The Complete Illustrated Sherlock Holmes* for my birthday then Dad would still be alive. Probably.

It was my tenth birthday, I think. Or maybe eleventh. Some time around then. I don't remember who gave it to me. It couldn't have been Mom, she was long since gone. And I know it wasn't Dad, because he always forgot my birthday. The only thing he ever gave me was dirty washing and a sore head. Anyway, it doesn't make any difference who gave it to me as long as someone did. Which they did. *The Complete Illustrated Sherlock Holmes*. It was a huge, thick book containing all the Sherlock Holmes stories and illustrated with the original drawings showing Sherlock as this gaunt and scary figure with crazy, sunken eyes and a cruel mouth. I'd never read any mystery stories before and I probably wouldn't have bothered then if I hadn't been stuck in bed with a virus. I mean, it was a *really* thick book, nearly a thousand pages. That's a lot of pages. It weighed a ton. But I got so bored just lying around in bed doing nothing, staring at the walls, listening to the sound of Dad clomping around in a drunken daze, cursing because he had to make his own dinner, I got so bored that I picked up this huge book one day and just started to read. And it was brilliant. I couldn't put it down. I loved it, every single story. A thousand pages? Nowhere near enough. I was hooked. Mystery after mystery after mystery. I read the whole lot in two days. Then I read them all again.

And that's how I came to love mystery stories. Murder mysteries, crime novels, whodunits, thrillers, detective stories, call them what you like, I love them.

After I'd put all the shopping away, then cleaned up a bit and did the dishes and made Dad some cheese on toast, I went up to my room and lay on the bed and tried to read for a while. *The Big Sleep* by Raymond Chandler. In case you don't know, Raymond Chandler is the best detective writer ever. Philip Marlowe, that's who he writes about. Marlowe, Private Investigator. Cool, tough, bitter, and funny. A man of honor. Mean streets. Mean villains. Mean city. Bad girls, good girls, crazy girls. Good cops, bad cops. Smart dialogue. Blackmail, murder, mystery, and suspense. And a plot with more twists than a snake with a bellyache. I'd read all the other Marlowe stories and I'd been looking forward to reading *The Big Sleep* for ages. It's supposed to be his best. But when I opened it up and started to read, I just couldn't get going. The words wouldn't stick. I'd get to the bottom of the page then realize I couldn't remember anything I'd just read. So I'd start again, concentrating, making sure I read every line, every word, one at a time, nice and slow, and then halfway through I'd lose it again. I don't know. It was like I had no control over my thoughts, they'd just drift off somewhere without my knowing. So, I gave up on the book and just lay there on the bed, staring blindly at the ceiling.

I thought about Alex. I was looking forward to seeing her later that evening. She came over most evenings. Sometimes I'd go over to her place, but mostly she came to mine. We didn't do anything, just sat around talking. I remember the very first time she came around, about a week after we'd first met, I didn't know what to think. I was in quite a state. Why was she coming? What did she want? Did she like me? What should I do? I was a nervous wreck. But when she showed up it was as if we'd known each other for years. No problem. No uneasiness. No awkward undertones. She didn't even seem too bothered about Dad.

"Is he always drunk?" she'd asked, after he'd stumbled through the bedroom door, eyed her up, winked at me like a lecher, then stumbled out again.

"Just about."

"Mine was like that," she said matter-of-factly. "That's why Mom got rid of him."

Her mom was an actress. She'd had a part in a daytime soap about fifteen years ago. I don't remember the name of it. It was something about a clothes store, or a factory or something. Anyway, she was in it for about a year.

"She was quite well known for a while," Alex told me. "Not famous, exactly, sort of semi-famous."

"Like what's-her-name from thingy?"

"Who?"

I smiled.

"Oh, right," she said. "Yeah, like that. People used to come up to her and say, "You're that one on that TV show, aren't you? You're . . . no, don't tell me, it's on the tip of my tongue . . . don't tell me. . . ."

"And what was it?"

"What?"

"Her name."

"Shirley Tucker!" She laughed. "A sexy young blond with a heart of gold. Mom had to wear this great big wig, you know, with loads of makeup, short skirts, and everything. She looked great. Anyway, a couple of years after I was born Shirley and her boyfriend were *tragically killed* in a motorcycle accident . . . and since then Mom's found it really hard to find any steady work. She still gets the odd acting job now and then — local theater, commercials, the occasional bit part on TV, that sort of thing — but it's not enough to pay the rent, so she's had to go back to part-time nursing. She hates it."

"Why did they kill off her character?"

"I don't know . . . and there was something . . . a disagreement with the producers or something. Mom doesn't like talking about it."

Over the next few weeks we talked about everything. Alex told me all about herself, where she was from, what she thought about stuff, what she wanted to do.

"I'm going to be an actress, too," she told me. "Mom was dead against it at first, she kept on telling me I ought to be a lawyer or something. 'That's where the money is, Alex, there's no such thing as a poor lawyer, you know.' But once she realized I was serious about acting she changed her mind, and now she really helps me. She's brilliant, Martyn, you ought to see her. She just has to raise an eyebrow and she becomes a different person. She can do anything: voices, the way people walk, their posture, anything. She's brilliant."

I thought of asking: If she's so good, how come she can't get a job? But I didn't. I didn't want to spoil the atmosphere. And in any case, I was genuinely impressed. Even if she wasn't semi-famous anymore, at least Alex's mom had done *something*. All right, so she was a has-been. But a has-been is better than a never-has-been-and-never-will-be, like Dad. And Alex was so proud of her. It was such an alien concept — being proud of someone — I couldn't help but be impressed. But what impressed me most about Alex was her ambition. She had an *ambition*. She knew what she wanted to do, she wanted to *be* something. And she was good, too. A good actress, I mean. "Tell me what you want me to be and I'll be it," she said once.

"What do you mean?"

"Anything," she said. "A situation, an emotion, a person . . . anything." She flapped her arms in an elaborately dramatic gesture and put on an actory voice, "I will *act* for you."

"Anger," I suggested.

"Can't you think of anything better than *that*?"

"Well, I. . . ."

Her rage disappeared and she grinned. "Acting, Martyn. I was acting. Anger."

"Yeah," I mumbled. "I knew that."

"No you didn't. Give me another. A person."

I thought for a moment, then smiled. "My dad."

"OK. Just a minute." She was sitting cross-legged on the bed. She closed her eyes, muttered under her breath for a while, then got up and loped across the room and went out the door. I thought she'd gone to the bathroom. Just then there was a heavy knock on the door followed by a deep slurred voice. "Mar'n! Mar'n! Get down 'ere and make me some coffee!"

I answered without thinking. "Yeah, OK, Dad."

The door opened and Alex came in grinning triumphantly. "And don't take all bloody day about it, neither."

It was uncanny. She sounded *just* like him.

"Amazing," I said. "Incredible."

She licked her little finger and groomed an eyebrow. "It was nothing, a mere trifle."

Ambition *and* talent . . . it was beyond me.

"What about you, Martyn?" she asked me. "What do you want to do? What do you want to be?"

What did I want to be? I'd never even thought about it. What did I want to do? All I wanted to do was something else. Something that wasn't what I was doing. Whatever that was. Nothing much. What did I want to be? What kind of question is that? *What did I want to be?* God knows.

I said the first thing that came into my head. "I want to be a writer. I'm going to write a murder mystery."

"Really?"

"Yeah. They'll make it into a television series and I'll make loads of money."

"I hope there's a part in it for me. And my mom."

"The ghost of Shirley Tucker?"

"Yeah!"

"OK. And who do *you* want to be?"

She thought about that for a while, then said, "The murderer's beautiful mistress."

"Why?"

She shrugged and smiled. "Why not?"

One thing we didn't talk about much was Dean. A few weeks after she'd started seeing him, after I'd met him for the first time, I asked her why she was going out with him.

"What do you mean?" she said.

"Well . . ."

"Well what?"

"Well . . . he's a bit of a dope, isn't he?"

She went nuts. "How the hell would you know what he's like! You've only met him *once*."

"I didn't mean —"

"You didn't mean *what*? What's it got to do with *you*, anyway? Who the hell d'you think you are?"

I apologized as best I could but she didn't want to know. She sulked for a couple of days, kept out of my way, didn't come around for a while. I thought I'd blown it. Then, all of a sudden, she just seemed to forget all about it. She came over one night and everything was back to normal, as if nothing had ever been said.

Still, we didn't talk about Dean much after that.

Dad was drunk when I went downstairs, which was no surprise. He was drunk every night. Sometimes he went out and sometimes he stayed in, but it didn't make any difference, he was drunk wherever he was. He drank during the day, too, kept himself liquored up with beer, but he never really got going on the hard stuff until the evening. Beer in the morning, beer for lunch, and beer in the afternoon. Then beer and whisky for an afternoon snack, and finally, whisky for supper. A balanced diet. He drank so much that even when he wasn't drinking he was drunk.

In the evening, after he'd started on the whisky, there were four distinct stages to his drunkenness. Stage One, the first hour or so after he'd started, he'd make out like he was my best pal — cracking jokes, ruffling my hair, asking how I was, giving me money.

"An'thing you need, Marty? 'Ere, 'ere's a coupla bucks, go on, get y'self a book or something."

I hate being called Marty. And I hated him giving me money. He'd always ask for it back the next day, anyway. When he was like this, trying to be funny, trying to be Mr. Nice Guy, I think that's when I hated him the most. I preferred him when he got to Stage Two. At least it was honest. Stage Two was mostly self-pitying misery. There'd be a silent interval between Stage One and Stage Two, then the occasional grunt at something on television or something in the newspaper, then he'd gradually build up steam, cursing his ugly luck, cursing the injustices of this world, cursing this and cursing that, cursing Mom for deserting him, cursing Aunty Jean for being such a witch, cursing me for tying him down with responsibilities, cursing just about everything that wasn't him, basically. Then, all at once, he'd just stop, and for the next hour or so he'd just sit there slumped in his chair, smoking his cigarettes, and pouring whisky down his neck until he got to Stage Three. Stage Three was incoherence with an unpredictable hint of violence. It didn't bother me too much, the violence, not once I'd learned how to cope with it. It wasn't difficult, really. It usually started with a question. The trick was to give the right answer, but that wasn't always easy because it was almost impossible to understand what he was saying.

"I tellya, I tellya, lissen, 'mI doin' the bessacan or 'mI not? Y'thingiseasy? Y'thingiseasy? Y'thing I donwunna gi'y'thebess? Eh? Lissen. Y'thing I donwunna?"

If I gave the right answer he'd just leer at me for a second then start on about something else. But if I gave the wrong answer — like, "What?" — then he'd more than likely swing at me. But, like I said, it didn't really matter. Most times he was so incapable that all I had to do was step to one side and he'd miss . . . most times. I remember once, though, we were sitting at the table eating dinner and Dad had a cigarette smoking in the ashtray. The smoke was getting all over the place, stinking up the food, getting in my eyes, making me cough. I kept on asking him to move it, but he just sat there reading his paper, ignoring me, so finally I reached across to move it myself — and his fist came down like a hammer. Whack. Broke my wrist. I couldn't believe it. I'd never seen him move so fast in his life. When he realized what he'd done and that I'd have to go to the hospital, he started getting really worried.

"Was a acc'dent, Mar'n. Was a acc'dent. Y'gotta tell'em. Was a acc'dent."

What it was, he was worried they'd send the social worker around again. You see, earlier in the year, one of the teachers at school had noticed a particularly nasty bruise on my arm. She started asking all these awkward questions — How did it happen? Is everything all right at home? Why are you so tired all the time? — that kind of thing. I tried to put her off but she wouldn't leave it alone, and in the end this social worker came around poking his nose into everything. Dad was shaking like a leaf. He thought they were going to cut off his benefit checks. But when the social worker talked to me I made out like everything was OK — which it was, in a way — and he seemed happy enough when he left. Of course, Dad put on his *ideal father* act for the next couple of days — smiling at me, talking to me, trying to be nice — but once he realized he was in the clear he was soon back to normal. Thank God. The way I looked at it, things weren't perfect, but at least I knew where I was with Dad. Better the devil you know than the devil you don't, as they say.

Maybe everything would have turned out different if I'd told the truth. But I didn't. When I went to the hospital with my broken wrist I told the doctor it was an accident, I fell off my bike.

So, anyway, that was Dad in Stage Three — incoherent with an unpredictable hint of violence. Stage Four — the final stage — was when he collapsed into a drunken coma. Anywhere would do. In his chair, on the floor, in the bathroom, on the toilet, lying wherever he fell, snorting out great snotty snores, all kinds of dribbly stuff oozing out of his mouth. The scariest thing was when he stopped snoring, just lay there as quiet as a dead man. Unwakeable. I poured a pan of cold water over his head once. He still didn't wake up. That's why I took a first aid course at school. So I could tell whether he was dead or just dead drunk.

That evening, either I'd misread how much he'd had to drink or else he'd jumped straight from Stage One to Stage Three. Or maybe something else happened. I don't know. I don't think about it much, to be honest.

All I was trying to do was watch *Inspector Morse* on television. Is that too much to ask? I hardly ever watch television. *Morse*, *Law and Order*, *NYPD Blue*, that kind of thing. *Dragnet* reruns, sometimes. That's all I watch, that's what I like. Detective stuff. Mysteries, murder mysteries. I love them. Especially *Morse*. I'm not too keen on the books, but the television series is amazing. Two hours each. Amazing. What more could a budding murder mystery writer ask for? Two hours of twisting plots, red herrings, strange priests, spooky murderers, and good old Morse always getting it right in the end.

Now, with *Morse*, you have to really watch it. From start to finish. It's no good just having the television on in the background, watching a bit here and a bit there; you have to concentrate all the way through. Otherwise you won't have a clue what's going on. And if you don't know what's going on, there's no point in watching it.

So, Wednesday night. Eight-thirty. In the front room. The curtains were closed. A cold orange light was flickering behind the false coal of the electric fire. I was sitting on the floor with my back against the couch and Dad was in his armchair, drinking. I didn't know how many he'd had, but I didn't think it was that many because he kept on making stupid jokes about *Morse*, trying to be funny. Stage One. It was annoying, but I just sat there trying to ignore him in the hope that he'd get bored and shut up, or go down to the pub and leave me in peace. But he didn't. He kept on. Piping up every other minute with his pathetic comments.

"Look at him! He's getting a bit fat, isn't he?"

"Cops don't drive Jags!"

"No wonder he's so miserable, listening to that awful music all the time."

He just wouldn't stop. On and on and on. I couldn't concentrate. I couldn't hear what was going on. I was losing the plot.

Then he started with his Lewis thing.

Just in case you don't know who Lewis is, he's Morse's sidekick. Sergeant Lewis. A bit of a plodder, in contrast to Morse's unconventional genius. Once or twice in every episode Morse calls out Lewis's name: "*Lew-is!*" Kind of a catch phrase. For some inexplicable reason, Dad always found this hilarious, and whenever it happened he started calling out, too, calling out in a stupid imitation-Morse voice: "*Lew-is! Lew-is! Lew-is!*" And then he'd laugh like mad at his own incredible wit. The first time he did it, it was almost amusing. Almost, but not quite. But after hearing it about a hundred times since, it just made me sick. Why? Why did he do it? Over and over again. *Why?*

So there I was, sitting on the floor, leaning toward the television, trying to keep track of what was going on. Morse was in his office, sitting at his desk, pondering, frowning, trying to work out whodunit. Dreamy music was playing in the background. Suddenly, he sat up straight and blinked. Something had occurred to him. Something crucial. He got up and opened his door and called down the corridor for Lewis: "*Lew-is!*" And then Dad started. "*Lew-is! Lew-is! Lew-is! Lew-is!*" He wouldn't stop. "*Lew-is! Lew-is! Lew-is! Lew-is!*" And all the time he was snorting with laughter as if it was the funniest thing in the world. On the television Morse was talking to Lewis, explaining his crucial idea, but I couldn't hear a thing.

All I could hear was Dad's crazy braying in my ear: "*Lew-is! Lew-is! Lew-is! Lew-is! Lew-is! Lew-is! Lew —*"

"SHUT UP!"

I'd got to my feet and was facing him across the room. "For God's sake, Dad, just shut up! It's not funny, it's pathetic. You're pathetic. Why can't you just shut your mouth and let me watch the television for once?"

He stared at me, stunned. I stared back at him. He put his beer can down on the table. "*What* did you say?"

"Nothing. It doesn't matter."

My anger had gone. I turned away.

I sensed, rather than heard, the movement behind me, and I turned just in time to see him bearing down on me with his fist raised above his head and drunken madness burning in his eyes.

My reaction was automatic. As I jumped to one side the downward surge of his fist missed my head by a whisker. Then, as his momentum carried him past me, I shoved him in the back. That's all it was, a shove. Just a shove. An instinctive defensive gesture. No more. I didn't hit him or anything. All I did was push him away. I barely *touched* him. He must have been off balance, I suppose. Too drunk to stay on his feet. Legless. I don't know. . . . All I know for sure is that he flew across the room and smacked his head into the fireplace wall then fell to the hearth and was still. I can still hear the sound of it now. That sickening crack of bone on stone.

I knew he was dead. Instantly. I knew.

Do you see what I mean now, about *The Complete Illustrated Sherlock Holmes*? If I'd never been given it for my birthday, if I'd never read it, then I'd never have fallen in love with murder mysteries. And if I'd never fallen in love with murder mysteries then I wouldn't have been watching *Inspector Morse* on the television. And if I hadn't been watching *Inspector Morse* on the television, Dad wouldn't have been sitting there shouting "*Lewis! Lew-is! Lew-is!*" like a madman and I wouldn't have got annoyed and I wouldn't have told him to shut up and he wouldn't have tried to bash my head in and I wouldn't have shoved him in the back and he wouldn't have hit his head against the fireplace and died.

The thing is, though . . . the thing is, if you look at it that way, if you follow that line of reasoning, then it was all his fault in the first place. If he hadn't been my father, you know, if he hadn't impregnated Mom, then I would never have been born. I wouldn't have existed. And he would still be alive. It was *his* fault that I existed. He made me. I never *asked* to be born, did I? It was nothing to do with me.

But then again, it wasn't *his* fault that *he* was born, was it?

I don't know.

Does there have to be a reason for everything?

I knew he was dead. I could feel it. The air, the flatness, the lifelessness.

I stood motionless for a minute. Just stood there, staring, my mind blank, my heart beating hard. It's strange, the lack of emotion, the absence of drama in reality. When things happen in real life, extraordinary things, there's no music, there's no *dah-dah-daaahhs*. There's no close-ups. No dramatic camera angles. Nothing happens. Nothing stops, the rest of the world goes on. As I was standing there in the front room, looking down at the awkwardness of Dad's dead body lying on the hearth, the television just carried on jabbering away in the background. Ads. Happy families dancing around a kitchen table: *I feel like chicken tonight, I feel like chicken tonight.* . . . I leaned down and switched it off. The silence was cold and deathly.

"My God," I whispered.

I had to check. Even though I knew he was dead, I had to make sure. I stepped over to the fireplace and squatted down beside him. An ugly dark wound cut into the bone just above his eye. There wasn't much blood. A crimson scrape on the fireplace wall, a smear on the hearth that was already drying. I looked closer. A thin red ribbon meandered down from the corner of his mouth and lost itself in the dark stubble of his chin. I looked into his lifeless face. You can tell. Even if you've never seen a dead body before, you can tell. The appearance of death cannot be mistaken for unconsciousness. That gray-white pallor. Flat and toneless. Without essence. The skin sheenless and somehow shrunken, as if whatever it is that *is* life — the spirit, the soul — has been stripped away and all that's left is an empty sack. I looked into his glassy black eyes and they stared blindly back at me.

"You stupid bastard," I said quietly.

I lightly placed a finger on his neck. Nothing. No pulse. Then I loosened buttons on his shirt and lowered my ear to his chest, listening, without hope, for the sound of his heart. There was no sound.

I know what you're thinking. Why didn't I call 911, call an ambulance? They could have revived him. Just because someone's stopped breathing, it doesn't necessarily mean they're dead, does it? Why didn't you give him artificial respiration? You studied first aid, didn't you? Why didn't you try to save his life?

I don't know.

Why didn't I try to save his life?

I don't know. I just didn't.

All right?

Well, anyway, that's what happened. Make of it what you like. I don't really care. I was there. It happened. I know it.

After I'd made sure he was dead I went over and sat in Dad's armchair. Which was kind of an odd thing to do, because I'd never sat there before. Ever.

I sat there for a long time.

A long time.

I suppose I must have been thinking. Or maybe not. I don't know. I don't remember. I just remember sitting there, alone in the evening silence, enshrined behind closed curtains, alone with the careless *tick-tock*ing of the clock on the mantel. I think that was the first time I'd ever heard it.

The harsh clatter of rain jerked me out of my trance. It was ten o'clock. I stood up and rubbed my eyes, then went over to the window and pulled back the curtain. It was pouring down. Great sheets of rain lashing down into the street. I closed the curtain again and turned around. There he was. My dead dad. Still dead. Still buckled over, sprawled across the hearth like a broken doll. The buttons on his shirt were still undone where I'd listened at his heart. I stooped down and did them up again.

An image suddenly flashed into my mind — one of those chalk outlines that detectives draw around the murder victim's body. It amused me, for some reason, and I let out a short, strangled laugh. It sounded like someone else, like the sound of laughter echoing in a ghost town.

I sat down again.

What are you going to do? I asked myself.

The telephone on the table by the door sat there black and silent, waiting. I knew what I *ought* to do.

Wind-blown sheets of rain were rattling against the window. The room was cold. I was shivering. I shoved my hands deep down into my pockets.

This was a sweet mess.

The doorbell rang.

It was Alex, of course. No one else ever came around to our house, no one except for debt collectors and Mormons. And Aunty Jean once a year.

I let Alex in, closed the front door, and took her into the kitchen. She looked wonderful. Her hair was bunched up on the top of her head, tied with a light-blue ribbon, and one or two fine black strands hung rain-wet and loose down the pale curve of her neck. Her face . . . Alex's face. It was so pretty. Fine. Perfect. A pretty girl's face. Her teeth were white as mints. She was wearing the same clothes she'd been wearing that afternoon at the bus stop — army jacket, white T-shirt, old blue jeans. All wet through.

She put her bag on the table and wiped a mist of rain from her brow. "Where's your dad?"

"In the front room," I said. "Do you want some tea?"

I put the kettle on and sorted out the mugs and tea things while Alex sat down at the kitchen table, rubbing some warmth into her arms. "It's a bit cold in here, isn't it?"

The kettle boiled and I filled two mugs.

"Enjoy yourself?" I asked.

She shrugged. "It was all right."

"Where'd you go?"

"Nowhere. Dean was fooling around with some stuff from the shop, tape recorders, computer stuff, I don't know."

I fished the teabags from the mugs and threw them at the trash can but they missed and splatted onto the floor. I added milk to the tea.

"Alex?"

"What?"

I put the teas on the kitchen table and sat down.

"I've got a problem," I said.

"You're not pregnant, are you?" she joked.

"No."

"Sorry." She stopped smiling. "What is it? Is it bad?"

"It's bad."

"How bad?"

"*Bad* bad."

"Oh."

"It's Dad."

"What about him?"

"He's dead."

And then I told her what had happened.

• • •

"Show me," she said.

I took her into the front room. She shuddered a little and wiped nervously at her mouth.

"Cover him up, Martyn."

I found a sheet in the closet and laid it over the body.

"Come here," she said gently.

I moved over to her and she put her arms around me. Her skin smelled of rain.

That moment, when she held me . . . it was as if nothing else mattered. Nothing. Everything would be all right. Her soft hand on the back of my head, the comfort of her body close to mine . . . everything else just faded away into nowhere. This was where I wanted to be.

But nothing lasts forever.

Back in the kitchen she just sat there looking at me. Flecks of green dappled the brown of her eyes, like tiny leaves. I had to look away. My tea was cold. Everything was cold.

"You have to tell somebody," she said quietly.

The fluorescent strip light hummed and stuttered on the ceiling. A small puddle of rainwater had formed on the floor at Alex's feet, dripped from the sleeves of her jacket. The harsh white flickering light reflected in the surface of the puddle. It bothered me. I wanted to turn it off. To sit in the dark. To do nothing.

"Martyn, you have to tell somebody about it. You can't just sit here and not do anything. You have to call the police."

"I can't."

"Why not?"

"It's too late."

A frown wrinkled her brow. "I don't understand. Too late for what?"

"They'll know."

"Who?"

"The police. They'll know he died over an hour ago. They can tell. They'll want to know why I didn't call right away."

"So? Tell them."

"I can't, can I?"

"Why not?"

"Because I don't know."

"Oh." She looked down, a little embarrassed, as if she'd suddenly realized there was something wrong with me. She had that don't-know-what-to-do look on her face, the kind of look you get when a crazy person sits next to you on a bus. But it didn't last long. After a moment's thought she wiped her nose and said, "Well, all right, but you're not going to get arrested just because you don't know why you didn't do something, are you?"

"No, they'll probably just put me in a loony bin."

"Don't be stupid."

"Or a home, or something."

"Martyn —"

"They won't let me stay here, will they?" And then it dawned on me. "Oh, God. Aunty Jean. They'll make me go and live at Aunty Jean's."

"No they won't."

"Of course they will! What else can they do? Christ! I can't live with her, I can't *stand* the woman. She's worse than Dad."

39

"I'm sure it's not *that* bad."

"How would *you* know?" I snapped.

She looked hurt. "I'm only trying to help."

"Yeah, I know . . . I know. I'm sorry. It's just . . . I don't know."

It was still pouring down. Rain streamed on the kitchen window. The shaving cream snow had melted. All that was left was a murky trail on the glass and a grubby white residue hardening on the sill. Alex scratched absently at the tabletop with a teaspoon, chewing her lip, while I just sat there thinking. It was one of those *if only* situations. If only no one knew about it. If only I had time to think. If only I could make things disappear. If only . . .

"Look," Alex said calmly, "why don't you let me call the police. I'll explain what's happened. I'm sure it'll be all right. I mean, it's not like he's been lying there for weeks, is it? It's only been an hour or so. They'll understand, they're not monsters."

I shook my head.

"Why not?"

"I've already *told* you, they'll want to know why I didn't tell them about it immediately, and I won't have an answer. It's bound to make them suspicious. They'll think I've got something to hide."

"Yes, but you haven't, have you? It was an accident."

"They don't know that."

"But you can't just *leave* it, Martyn. You've got to do something. You've got to tell *some*body."

I thought about it. I tried to follow it through — what if this, what if that — but there was nothing there. All I could see was a black hole. "Anyway," I said, "whatever I do, I'll still end up at Aunty Jean's."

"But you won't have to stay there forever, will you? You'll be sixteen soon enough, you can get your own place."

"I'll be in a straitjacket by then."

"And what do you think's going to happen if you leave your dad's body in the front room?"

I looked at her. "I don't know."

She took a deep breath and sighed.

And that's how it went on for the rest of the night. Alex saying call the police and me saying no. Alex saying why not and me saying I can't. Why not? Because. Yes, but. No. Why not? Because. Yes, but. No . . . Around and around in never-ending circles. We weren't getting anywhere. By the time it got to midnight we were both too tired to carry on.

"Let's talk about it tomorrow," I said finally.

"It's already tomorrow. The longer you leave it —"

"I know. Let me think about it, OK? I'll sort it out in the morning."

She sighed again, looked at her watch, and nodded wearily. "All right."

I got up and went over to the back door. On the path outside, wet black garbage bags sagged by wall. Cats had got into one, scattering the path with wet tissue and chicken bones.

"What about tonight?" Alex said. "You can't stay here."

"I'll be all right."

"You can come over to my place if you want. I'll get Mom to make up a bed in the spare room."

"Thanks," I said, leaning on the door. "But I'll be all right here."

We were standing in the doorway. The rain had stopped. A crescent moon hung high and white in the black sky. The street was empty, the surface of the road wet and black in the glow of streetlights. Alex buttoned her coat.

"Are you sure you'll be all right?" she asked again.

I nodded.

She put her hands in her pockets. "I'd better go. I'll come over in the morning, OK?"

I watched her cross the road back to her house. Back to her home, her mother, her warm bed.

She didn't look back.

I shut the door.

The house was still cold. And quiet.

I went upstairs and got into bed.

THURSDAY

A small, windowless room lit by a naked lightbulb. Condensation gleams on bare concrete walls. On a shelf by the wall twin cassette tapes whirr in a big black tape recorder, red light blinking automatically.

It's cold, but my hands are sweating.

Across the table from where I sit, Inspector Morse shakes his head impatiently.

"I don't have *time* for this, Pig. What did you do with the gun?"

Standing behind him, wearing a long coat and a deerstalker hat, cradling his angular chin in his hand, Sherlock Holmes fixes me with a black-eyed stare. I look away and turn my attention back to Morse.

"What are you talking about?" I ask him. "What gun?"

"Oh come on, Pig," he says with exasperation, "I know you shot him. *Holmes* knows you shot him. We all *know* you shot him."

"Shot *who*? What are you talking about?"

He gives me his tight-mouthed look and rises from the chair. Sherlock leans over and whispers something in his ear. Morse grins and sits down again.

"Where were you at eight-thirty this evening?"

"At home. Watching television."

"Watching what?"

"Watching you."

"Why did you shoot your father?"

"I didn't shoot him. It was an accident —"

"That's not what Alex says."

"What?"

"Alex says you shot him."

"She wasn't there!"

"That's what *you* say."

"It's the truth!"

"Where were you at eight-thirty this evening?"

"Watching television."

"Watching what?"

"Watching you!"

"*Lew-is!*"

Morse's face shifts eerily as he shouts, changing into something else.

"*Lew-is! Lew-is!*"

His silvery-gray hair darkens, glinting with oil.

"*Lew-is! Lew-is!*"

A blackened wound appears on his forehead.

He won't stop shouting. "*Lew-is! Lew-is!*"

Blood seeps from the corner of his mouth.

"Lew-is! Lew-is! Lew-is! Lew-is!"

"SHUT UP!"

I sat up screaming vainly into the darkness. It was four o'clock in the morning.

The thing about dreams, they don't come from anywhere else but yourself. It's not as if there's some evil demon waiting around somewhere, waiting for you to sleep so he can sneak into your mind and show you all his crazy things. It's you that does it. It's your mind. Whatever demons there are, you invite them in. They're *your* demons. No one else's.

I don't know what that means.

I couldn't get back to sleep so I decided to take a bath. I felt dirty. My skin itched, sticky with sweat. And my legs ached, too. My legs always ache in the morning. Growing pains.

I shut the bathroom door and turned on the taps. The water gurgled and spat for a while, stopped, then coughed into life. I sat down on the toilet and waited for the bath to fill. My reflection looked back at me from the mirror on the wall.

"What?" I said.

The head reflected in the steamed glass was unmoved.

What I saw was a boy who didn't seem to fit his body. Thin. Gawky. Awkward. A shock of mud-brown hair, cut in no recognizable style, tired blue eyes, a too-small nose, and a crooked mouth with slightly crooked teeth. I was no beauty. But then again, I wasn't exactly a hunchback, either. Odd-looking? Maybe. But what's wrong with that?

The bath was nearly full. I opened a bottle of shampoo and squirted it into the bath. I watched the froth of rainbowed bubbles rise from the surface of the water like a perfumed mountain. Then I turned off the taps and stepped into the bath and lay there soaking and sweating in the silent heat of the water.

I lay there until it turned flat and cold. And then I lay there some more.

Thinking.

What could I do? What do you do when you don't know what to do? Cry? Scream? Run away? Feel sorry for yourself?

What's the point? There's always an answer somewhere. You've just got to find it.

I brushed my teeth. I dressed in clean clothes and ran a towel over my hair. I cleaned the sink, wiped the shelves, opened the window to let in some fresh air. It was still dark outside. A solitary bird whistled from somewhere hidden — *tsui-tsui-tsui*.

"What the hell," I said, and went downstairs.

Dabbing at toast crumbs and sipping tea, I watched through the window as the sun rose slowly and nudged away the dead cold blackness of the night. It wasn't much to see, the birth of another gray day, but I watched it, anyway. When it was done I looked at the clock and saw that it was still early.

I made some more tea.

I felt as if I was waiting for something, but I didn't know what it was.

What happened next, I suppose you'd call it fate. Whatever that is. I remember once one of the teachers at school started talking about destiny — fate, determinism, free will — that sort of thing. Mr. Smith, it was, the English teacher. "Call me Brian," he used to say, but no one ever did. It was pretty weird stuff, what he talked about, but it was kind of interesting, too. I spent a couple of days looking into it, getting books out of the library, reading this and reading that. But I didn't find out all that much because it's one of those things that doesn't really go anywhere because no one knows the answers. There aren't any answers. All that happens is the further you look into it, the more confusing it gets. So I stopped.

One thing that did stick in my mind, though, was something that Albert Einstein once said. I like him, Einstein. He's the crazy-haired one who thought up relativity. *Everything is determined,* he said, *the beginning as well as the end, by forces over which we have no control. It is determined for the insect as well as for the star. Human beings, vegetables, or cosmic dust, we all dance to a mysterious tune, intoned in the distance by an invisible piper.*

I thought that was pretty good.

The invisible piper on this occasion was the mailman.

It must have been about eight o'clock when the mail rattled through the mail slot. Bills, junk mail, catalog stuff. Dad liked to order things from catalogs. Gardening equipment, tools, pens, radios, Elvis Presley clocks, shirts, hats, anything. When the stuff was delivered he'd hide upstairs so the delivery man would have to leave whatever it was around the back and Dad wouldn't have to sign for it. Then he'd claim that he never received what he'd ordered and he'd sell the stuff down at the pub. He even sold a computer once. Two computers, come to think of it. They sent a replacement for the one he said had never arrived and he sold that, too.

Among all the rubbish there was an envelope addressed to

Mr. William Pig, Esq., that caught my eye. It looked official. Handwritten, that old-fashioned, slopey kind of writing, with a fountain pen. I chucked the rest of the mail in the trash and went back into the kitchen, sat down at the table, and opened the letter.

Dear Mr. Pig, it began. *Further to our meeting on December first, I write to confirm that, as requested, a check in the amount of $60,000 was paid into your account this morning, being full payment of the bequest made to yourself in the last will and testament of Miss Eileen Pig. . . .*

I put the letter down, blinked, and picked it up again.

. . . $60,000 . . . being full payment of the bequest made to yourself in the last will and testament of Miss Eileen Pig. . . .

A six followed by four zeros. Sixty thousand. Sixty thousand dollars. I read on.

. . . blah blah blah do not hesitate to contact us . . . blah blah blah . . . further advice . . . blah blah blah . . . Yours sincerely, signed *M. Squiggle, Malcolm G. Elliott LL.B (Hons) Lawyer.*

$60,000.

A six and four zeros.

Sixty thousand dollars.

I couldn't believe it.

Who the hell was Eileen Pig?

Sixty thousand dollars? Dad had never mentioned *anything*. He must have known about this for ages. He wasn't going to tell me.

He wasn't going to tell me.

I stared at the letter again. It was dated Wednesday, December eighteenth. Yesterday. Sixty thousand dollars. Paid into his account. And he wasn't going to tell me. I couldn't believe it.

Someone, some relative, leaves him sixty thousand dollars in her will — and he was going to keep it to himself. It was so sick it was funny.

I went into the front room.

"Dad?"

He didn't answer.

I held out the letter toward him. "What were you going to do with this? Leave me? Take off somewhere on your own, drink yourself to death on a beach in the Bahamas, and leave me to Aunty Jean?"

He still didn't answer.

"Why didn't you *tell* me?" I shouted.

The sound of my voice, trembling, close to tears, rang out flat and dull in the dead air. I sat down in the armchair and sighed. The silence was true. Dad was never going to tell me anything. He was just a shape beneath a white shroud.

I folded the letter into my pocket and went upstairs.

Dad's room was a mess. Curls of wallpaper peeled from the walls revealing old layers of sick-yellow paint. Magazines littered the floor, mostly girly mags and copies of *Pick-n-Save*. A few paperback books, too — Westerns, stupid romances. I kicked them all into a pile. The bed — a big high thing with a solid wood headboard — was unmade and smelled unwashed. Bits of broken cookies and bread crumbs lay scattered beneath the duvet and three whitish pillows were scrunched up against the headboard, each one discolored with the stain of Dad's hair oil.

I sat on the edge of the bed and looked around. I hadn't been in here for a long time, not since Mom had left. I used to come in early Christmas morning to get my presents. Dad would still be asleep, head beneath the blankets, snoring off the Christmas Eve drinks, but Mom would be awake, rubbing the sleep from her eyes, smiling. I'd sit at the bottom of the bed, barely able to control my excitement, as she reached down under the bed and brought out presents wrapped in gold and silver paper and tied with ribbon. Boxes, packages, all kinds of shapes and sizes. All for me. *Lego*, a football, Matchbox racecars. . . .

Did that really happen?

It was hard to imagine now.

On the bedside table was a nightlight, a packet of cigarettes, an ashtray, and a beer glass half-filled with dusty water. The ashtray stank. There was a bureau on one side of the room and a wardrobe by the window. A trail of discarded clothes led from the bed to the wardrobe — pants, socks, a vest, crumpled trousers and shirts. A burger box lay half-hidden beneath a dirty undershirt. Two halves of a burger bun, hard and stale and burgerless, crusty and forgotten.

I stood up and went over to the bureau. A dinner plate and knife and fork sat on top, encrusted with remnants of dried food. The orangy-brown smear told me it was baked beans mopped up with a slice of bread. The bureau was locked. I reached for the knife and jammed it into the bureau door and levered down. The door snapped open. Inside, it was a mess: loose papers scattered all over the place, a handful of letters, leaky pens, a folded checkbook and bank card, a spilled ashtray, more crumbs, a whisky tumbler, a rusty old tin box. . . .

I sat down and went through the papers. It didn't take long; there wasn't much there — unpaid bills, old insurance stuff, birth and marriage certificates, a medical card. I sorted these into a pile and turned to the letters. There was one from a woman called Maeve. Stapled to the top was a clipping from a personal ad magazine: *EASYGOING 50'S FEMALE, slim and attractive, seeks younger male, 35–40, for dances and drinks. Photo appreciated.* The letter from Maeve thanked Dad for his offer, but no thanks.

The rest of the letters were all from Malcolm G. Elliott, Lawyer, and told the story of Eileen Pig, deceased. Apparently she was Dad's aunt. She'd immigrated to Australia about forty years ago and no one had seen or heard from her since. She'd died in some kind of home. A touch insane, from the sound of it, which was probably why she'd left Dad the money. And that was about it, end of story. I don't know why I'd bothered, really. I secured the letters with a rubber band and tidied them away, then nosed around through the rest of the stuff. The checkbook was half full. I leafed through the stubs, curious to see what he'd written checks for, but Dad's writing was illegible. The only one I could make out was in my handwriting: *Beer Tent — $15.00.* The bank card was still valid. The PIN number was written on the back in felt-tip pen. Good thinking, Dad.

The tin box was full of old photographs. Most of them were of Dad when he was a young man. In a pub with his friends, red-eyed, raising his glass to the camera; at the beach with a stupid-looking girlfriend; laughing, sticking a cigarette up his nose. There were none of me. And just one of Mom, a faded wedding photograph folded away at the bottom of the tin. Mom and Dad cutting the cake. I took it out for a closer look. Mom looked nervous. She was so young. About eighteen, I suppose. Her wedding dress didn't seem to fit properly and her veil was all cockeyed, but she still looked nice. Shiny black hair, pale face, dark eyes, that slightly crooked smile . . . she was beautiful. Dad was dressed in a too-tight suit, his face half-shadowed, and his hair slicked back with enough oil to fill a barrel. He looked like a gangster. There was empty space all around him, as if no one wanted to get too close. An exclusion zone. Even Mom was leaning away from him as he lurched toward the camera with a boozy leer on his face stabbing into the wedding cake with a long carving knife.

It felt strange, holding the photograph in my hand, feeling the dull shine of the paper, gazing into the depths of the image. That's him, I thought. That was Dad. Then, all those years ago. Is it the same person? Was it the same person, the same thing? And where was I in that time before I ever existed. Where was I then? What was I? Was I nothing, no thing at all? A non-existent thing? How could that be?

I put the photograph back in the box and shut the bureau.

Alex turned up a little later, about ten o'clock. By that time I'd washed the dishes, cleaned the kitchen floor, cleared away Dad's beer cans from the night before and emptied the ashtrays, vacuumed and sorted out all the washing. I was sitting in the kitchen when the doorbell rang. I had the radio on, NPR. I wasn't really listening but it was nice to hear the sound of quiet voices instead of the local radio racket I had to put up with when Dad was around.

As we moved past the front room into the kitchen, Alex glanced through the door and then looked away. I turned off the radio. She put her bag on the table and sat down with a sigh.

"This is ridiculous, Martyn. All of it. It's ridiculous. You can't go on like this. You've got to call the police. You can't just pretend that nothing's happened."

"It's not that easy."

"Oh, come on," she said. "Nobody's going to blame you for your dad's death. It was an accident. You didn't mean it. The police will understand that. All you've got to do is tell them what happened."

We were back on the same old stuff again. I said, "And how am I going to explain why it took me so long to report it? It's been over twelve hours, now."

She frowned. "I don't know . . . you panicked, you didn't know what to do, you were frightened. . . ."

"Traumatized?" I suggested.

"Right, you were traumatized. People do all sorts of strange things when they're in shock. It was a terrible experience. You were too shocked to think straight."

"For twelve hours?"

"Why not?"

I looked at her. "And what about you?"

"What *about* me?"

"What are you going to tell them?"

"What do you mean?"

"If I call the police they'll want to talk to you. They'll want to know why *you* didn't report it. They're going to find it hard to believe we were *both* too shocked to do anything."

Her eyes widened. "That's not fair!"

I shrugged. "It's true, though, isn't it? Put yourself in their shoes. There'll be an autopsy. They'll know that Dad died between eight-thirty and nine in the evening, yesterday, and they'll know that you were here—"

"How will they know *that*?"

"They'll ask you."

She licked her lips. "I could lie."

"Then I'd have to lie."

She stared at me with those big brown eyes. It was impossible to tell what she was thinking. I looked away and went over to the kitchen window. The sky was dull and silvery-gray. The color of Inspector Morse's hair. I grinned to myself, remembering my dream. *Where were you at eight-thirty this evening? Watching television. Watching what? Watching you.*

"What are you going to *do*, Martyn?"

I turned to face Alex. For the briefest of moments I didn't recognize her, she was a stranger. But almost immediately the illusion lifted. It must have been the light or something. She was nervously twisting a strand of hair in her fingers. "What are you going to do?" she repeated. "You can't just . . . what are you going to do with your dad? You can't just leave him where he is. . . . Martyn?"

I went over and sat down. "I've been thinking," I told her. "Maybe we could just put him somewhere."

"What do you mean?"

"Just put him somewhere." I shrugged. "Somewhere he won't be found."

She looked at me incredulously. "Put him somewhere? What do you mean? Put him *where*?"

"I don't know. Anywhere. A river, a lake, in the woods. A gravel pit."

She sat back in the chair. For a while she didn't say anything, just stared at the table. I waited. Eventually, she said, "You *are* joking, aren't you? I mean, even if you did put him somewhere, someone's bound to find him sooner or later."

"Probably."

"So what's the point?"

I smiled. "He's a drunk, Alex. *Was* a drunk. It wasn't unusual for him to go off drinking for days at a time and not come back."

"So?"

"So, all we have to do is get rid of the body somewhere, then, in a day or two, I'll call the police and tell them Dad's been missing since Wednesday. I'll just say he went out in the evening and never came back. Even if they do find him, they won't suspect me, will they? I'm just a kid."

Alex smiled dubiously. "So, all we have to do is get rid of the body? That's all, is it? Easy as that. Just get rid of the body."

"Why not?"

"Do you realize what you're saying?"

"Have you got a better idea?"

She leaned across the table and looked me in the eye. "Tell the police now, Martyn. Tell them what happened, just tell the truth."

I could feel the breath of her words on my skin, a faint whisper of something sweet. I looked at her. "If I tell the truth," I said, "I'll have to tell them everything. I won't be able to keep you out of it. Is that what you want?"

"No, but . . . I don't know."

I shook my head. "I can't call the police. Not now. It's too late. Too late for both of us. And, anyway —"

"What?"

I took the lawyer's letter from my pocket and laid it on the table. Alex looked at it, looked at me, then started to read. I stood up and went over to the window. Yellowy bits of cloud had crawled into the sky. It looked like a dirty handkerchief. I wiped a cloth over the draining board and stared through the glass. This house, this place where I lived, this street, this town; I hated it. Dirtygray. Dark and cold, everything too close. All the people living in dull acceptance of their misery, their drab surroundings. I hated it.

"Sixty thousand dollars," Alex said quietly.

I turned to her and smiled.

Look, he was already dead. I couldn't change that. I didn't mean it to happen, it just happened. It happened. All I was trying to do was make the best of it. I wasn't harming anyone. I wasn't hurting anybody. You can't hurt the dead, can you? I was just looking out for myself, that's all. What's wrong with that?

There's a deep, water-filled gravel pit hidden away down at the end of a narrow track at the old quarry on the other side of town. The place is abandoned. No one ever goes there. There's a pub about half a mile away. That's how I knew about it. Dad had left his wallet in the pub one night and the next day he'd sent me there to get it. I had to get a bus. On the way back, the next bus wasn't for more than an hour, so I decided to start walking. About half a mile up the road I came across this narrow track. Thinking it might be a shortcut I climbed the gate and followed the track down, but after a few minutes I realized it didn't go anywhere, just ended at this old gravel pit half-filled with stagnant black water.

"See," I explained to Alex, "even if they do find him, they'll assume he was in the pub, got drunk, then got lost walking home and fell into the gravel pit . . . bashed his head on something when he fell."

We were in my room, sharing a plate of cheese sandwiches. Stormy light filtered in through the window, highlighting clouds of dust particles that danced in the air as I paced back and forth.

"We'll need a car," I said. "Or a van or something."

Alex was quiet. Thoughtful.

"What about your mom's car?" I suggested. Alex wasn't old enough to drive but she sometimes "borrowed" her mom's car. It was one of those old VW Minibus things, a muddy-brown van held together with rust and dirt.

"I don't know," she said. "Maybe." She was sitting on the bed putting some kind of cream on her lips. She put the tube back in her bag and reached for a sandwich. "The car's at the garage until tomorrow," she explained, taking a bite.

"Tomorrow night, then."

"It might not be ready. If it needs a lot of work . . . I don't know if Mom can afford it."

"You're forgetting something," I said.

"What?"

"I've got sixty thousand bucks. I'm rich. I'll buy you a new car."

Alex sighed. "But the money's in the bank, in your dad's account."

I shrugged. "I've got his checkbook and bank card. . . . I'm sure we can work something out."

She shook her head. "I hope you know what you're doing."

"Don't worry about it." I reached for a sandwich. "So, what about the car?"

"I don't know. I'll have to find out what Mom's doing. Friday, maybe Saturday. I'll have to let you know."

We ate in silence. I liked to watch her eat. She took tiny

little bites and chewed each mouthful about a hundred times before she swallowed it.

"What?" she said, noticing me staring.

"Nothing."

I went to the bathroom. When I came back, Alex was still working on the same sandwich. I stood at the window. Heavy black clouds were looming in the distance, heaving themselves slowly through the sky like walruses crawling up a beach. Across the road, the woman from number seven was coming back from the stores, struggling up the pavement with a shopping bag dangling from each hand. She was about sixty. She always wore bright pink lipstick that smudged all over her teeth, and her dim eyes were decorated with thick daubs of purple eye shadow. Dad brought her back to the house once, after they'd met down at the pub. She was drunk, laughing like a hyena at everything Dad said. She'd started dancing at one point, doing the cancan, pulling up her skirt and flashing her long gray slip . . .

"Damn," I said.

"What?"

"Aunty Jean."

"What?"

"Aunty Jean's coming tomorrow. I just remembered."

"When?"

"Four o'clock."

"Can't you put her off? Say you're sick or something?"

"She's doesn't have a phone — well, she does, but she never answers it. She only uses it for making calls. The ringer's always switched off."

"Why?"

"I don't know. . . . It's just one of her crazy little ways. I think she's probably scared of talking to strangers."

"You're not a stranger."

"But she wouldn't know it was me, would she? I could be anyone."

"You could call first to let her know."

It was hard to tell if she was joking or not. Her face looked serious, but she could have been putting me on, acting stupid to trap me into correcting her. She did that sometimes. Then when I did correct her she'd smile to show me she was putting me on, and I'd feel stupid for having believed she could be so stupid. . . .

I wasn't in the mood for all that.

"She doesn't answer the phone," I said simply. "That's all there is to it."

"Well, you'll have to do something. She can't come here with your dad lying dead in the front room."

"No."

Things don't just happen, do they? They have effects. And the effects have effects. And the effects of the effects have effects. And then the effects of the things that happen make other things happen, so the effects of the effects become reasons. Nothing moves forward in a straight line, nothing is straight-forward.

The thought of Aunty Jean made my stomach turn. God, I thought, imagine it. Imagine living with *her*. She wouldn't leave you alone for a minute. There's no way she'd put up with your odd little ways. *What odd little ways?* You know what I mean.

And you can forget about Alex, too. A *girl*, Martyn? A girl? *How* old? Not in *my* house.

"I'm not going there," I said.

"What? Where?"

"Aunty Jean's. I'm not going there."

Alex looked puzzled. "I thought she was coming here."

Through the window I watched a bus pull away up the road. For an instant I thought I saw Alex sitting in the backseat. I thought I saw her turn and wave, smiling at me. Then the bus turned the corner and disappeared and I blinked and realized where I was. In this house. In this wretched house. I didn't have to stay here, did I? I could go somewhere else. Get the money, get out of here. We could go somewhere, me and Alex. Together. Anywhere. We could —

"I have to go," said Alex. "I'm meeting Dean at two."

Dean, Dean, Dean. Always blasted Dean.

"OK," I said.

"I'll try and think of something —"

"Yeah."

"I'll come over later. We'll talk some more. This evening. All right?"

"OK."

After she left I just kind of moped around for a while. Dad was starting to smell a bit. Kind of musty. The sort of smell you don't like but can't help sniffing at. Mind you, he always did stink a bit, even when he was alive, so I wasn't quite sure whether this musty smell was just an ordinary dirty-drunk-person-who-hasn't-washed-and-has-spent-the-night-lying-in-the-fireplace kind of smell, or if it was the start of something worse. I just didn't know. Not that there was much I could do about it, anyway. I gave the room a good going-over with air freshener, but that only made it worse. The whole house stank of musty flowers. I didn't want to open the windows in case the smell wafted out. Someone might notice it, someone who might recognize the smell of a dead body. You never know, do you? An undertaker might be walking past.

I went upstairs and put this morning's letter in the bureau with the others. While I was there I picked up Dad's bank card and took a good, long look at it. There was a hologram in the corner, a little silver square with a 3-D mug shot of Shakespeare on it. At least I think it was Shakespeare. A baldy-looking man with a beard and a big white collar. His head zipped around when I moved the card. It was weird. The slightest tilt and his expression changed. From a happy old guy with a twinkly smile — to a vicious madman with a cutthroat glare. Happy old guy — cutthroat glare. Happy old guy — cutthroat glare. Happy old guy — cutthroat glare. . . .

I got bored with that after a while and turned the card over. Dad's PIN number was 4514.

Morse would have made something of that.

Then the rain started again. I don't mind the rain. In fact, I like it. I like the way it pours down from the sky and makes everybody wet and panicky. I think it's funny. But this was something else. This was BIG rain. It was coming down in buckets. Pounding on the window. Gusting against the glass. Louder and louder. It wouldn't stop. I couldn't get it out of my head. It was so loud. So insistent. Pounding, pounding rain. Louder and louder and louder, like a thousand angry fingers rapping on the window.

I couldn't stand it.

I put the bank card back in the bureau, went to my room, and closed all the curtains. Then I got into bed, pulled the duvet over my head, and waited for the rain to stop.

I wasn't expecting Alex until later that evening so it was a pleasant surprise to hear the doorbell ring just after six o'clock. Even through the fluted glass in the front door her face was beautiful. Beautiful in distortion, like an angel in a hall of mirrors. I was smiling to myself as I opened the door — and then Dean stepped out from behind the wall, grinning, and my smile vanished.

"Hey, Pigman."

I stared at his unhealthy white skin, his baggy eyes, his stupid ponytail hanging down from his stupid fat head. I stared at his motorcycle jacket, shiny black leather, too-clean, too-new, and his black leather pants, baggy at the knees. I stared at the big black motorcycle helmet dangling from his hand, swinging gently, streetlights reflecting in its dark shine.

I stared at Alex. Dressed, like Dean, in black leather, with a helmet in her hand. How *could* you? I thought. How could you?

She looked down at her feet. "I'm sorry, Martyn."

What? *What?* Sorry? What do you mean, sorry? Sorry? *Sorry?*

Dean stepped up to the door and I went to close it.

"I wouldn't if I were you," he said.

The sound of his voice made me sick.

"He knows," said Alex.

"*What?*"

"He knows, Martyn. About your dad."

Something uncontrollable welled up inside me. Like a hurricane. A whirlwind of unwanted emotions. She'd betrayed me. She, Alex. *Alex.* She'd *betrayed* me. Me. Can you imagine that? Can you *feel* it?

Dean whistled a low whistle, shook his head, and grinned a cocky grin. "Unbelievable," he said. "Kids today, I don't know. No respect for their elders."

Alex was staring at me now, her eyes begging me to understand. And, strangely, I did. In an instant. I understood. She was scared. But not of me. Of him. She was scared of Dean. We were still in this together. Me and Alex.

Something inside me clicked off and the hurricane retreated. I stepped back and opened the door.

"You'd better come in."

"This is ridiculous, Martyn. All of it. It's ridiculous. . . ."

The minitape recorder whirred quietly on the kitchen table. I listened, dumbstruck, to the sound of Alex's voice.

"You can't go on like this. You've got to call the police. You can't just pretend that nothing's happened."

And then the sound of my own voice, oddly unfamiliar.

"It's not that easy."

"Oh, come on. Nobody's going to blame you for your dad's death. It was an accident. You didn't mean it. The police will understand that. All you've got to do is tell them what happened."

Dean smiled and pressed the fast forward button. I stared, transfixed, as the tape recorder's tiny wheels whizzed around. I heard the scrape of a match and looked up as Dean lit a cigarette.

"Want one?" he said.

I didn't answer. The smell of the smoke reminded me of Dad. The tape played on.

"Maybe we could just put him somewhere."

"What do you mean?"

"Just put him somewhere. Somewhere he won't be found."

"Put him somewhere? What do you mean? Put him where?"

"I don't know. Anywhere. A river, a lake, in the woods. A gravel pit."

A long silence.

Then: *"You are joking, aren't you? I mean, even if you did put him somewhere, someone's bound to find him sooner or later."*

"Probably."

"So what's the point?"

"He's a drunk, Alex. Was a drunk. It wasn't unusual for him to go off drinking for days at a time and not come back."

"So?"

"So all we have to do is get rid of the body somewhere, then, in a day or two, I'll call the police and tell them Dad's been missing since Wednesday. I'll just say he went out in the evening and never came back. Even if they do find him, they won't suspect me, will they? I'm just a kid. . . ."

I reached across the table and pressed the stop button.

"There's plenty more," said Dean. Cigarette smoke trailed languidly from his wide nostrils.

I looked across at Alex, standing by the window with her head bowed.

"Alex?"

She looked up, sad eyes glistening. "He bugged my bag."

"What?"

"A listening device. From the Gadget Shop. He put it in my bag. Yesterday. He taped us talking . . . everything." She was close to tears.

"Everything?"

She nodded.

Dean reached into his pocket and dropped a little electronic, buggy thing on the table — black plastic, about the size of a quarter, with a tiny metal grill on one side. "It's got a range of two miles," he said. "I linked up the receiver to a tape recorder." He picked up the bug and turned it over in his hand, smiling a self-satisfied smile. "Good, eh?"

"Why?" I asked him.

He stared at me across the table. There was something unsettling in his eyes. Something unbalanced.

"Why?" he repeated. "I was curious, that's why. You and Alex and your cozy little nighttime *talks*. I just wondered what you were up to, that's all. Know what I mean?" He turned to Alex. "You wouldn't tell me about your little Pigman, would you, Al?"

"It's none of your business, Dean, you don't *own* me."

He tapped the tape recorder and laughed. "I do now."

"What do you want?" I asked him.

He put the tape recorder in his pocket and drew on his cigarette. "All in good time, Piggy."

He was tall, nearly six feet, but stooped, as if his head weighed too much. I watched him straighten out his ponytail "Where's the body?" he asked.

"In the front room."

"Show me." The corner of his mouth twitched as he spoke, the tiniest of tics, and his left eyelid fluttered in reaction.

I led him into the front room and stepped aside to let him see.

He nodded at the shape beneath the sheet. "Is that it?"

"You want a look?"

He rubbed nervously at his jaw. "You do it. Lift the sheet."

"Scared?"

"Listen, Pig," he hissed, jabbing a long-nailed finger at me. "You do what I tell you and you just *might* get out of this in one piece. But you mess with me. . . ." He tapped the tape recorder in his pocket. "You mess with me and you'll end up in trouble. Get it? And her, too. In trouble." He sniffed. "All right?"

I said nothing.

"Lift the sheet," he said.

I walked across to the fireplace, bent down, and lifted a corner of the sheet. A pale dead head stared up at the ceiling. The black hair was dry and dull now, the sheen of oil dried, evaporated, gone. It wasn't Dad anymore, it wasn't even a person. It was just a dead thing, just a thing. I glanced at Dean. His pasty face was even pastier than usual, toneless and sallow. Even Dad looked healthier than that. A secret smile flickered in my mind as I squatted there. Look at him, I thought. He's nothing. A ponytailed zombie. Glazed, wasted-out blue eyes, dark pupils shrunk to almost nothing, small black holes floating in a watery nowhere. . . . He can't hurt me. I stared at him, hearing my voice in my head. You can't hurt me. You've got no strength, no purity. All you've got is cruelty and a streak of dumb cunning. That's not enough, that's not nearly enough. You know what your trouble is, Dean? You don't understand. You don't get it. You think that any of this really matters? You think I *care* what happens? To me, to anybody, to anything? I know it. I *know*. I know that nothing matters. That's what makes me strong. Strength in my own pure weakness.

No, I thought, you can't hurt me. But let's play the game, anyway.

I looked deeply into his eyes and smiled.

"Cover it up," he said.

I looked down at Dad, then back at Dean. "I think he likes you," I said.

"Cover it up!"

I let the sheet drop. Dean turned and went back into the kitchen, leaving me alone in the room. I took a deep breath and let it out slowly, trying to digest what I'd found in myself. It was good. A good feeling. Like I'd found my true self at last. What I was. I went over to the window and pulled back the curtain and gazed up into the night sky. No stars fell. The invisible piper was quiet this evening. There was nothing there, just the swoop of telephone wires hanging over the roofs of houses and a cold sliver of yellow moon. I nodded: nothing much at all, just the way it should be.

Alex had been crying, her eyes blurred and red. She was sitting at the kitchen table pulling a paper tissue to pieces. Dean was at the sink splashing cold water onto his face.

"It's all right," I told Alex. She looked up and I smiled. "Really," I said. "It's all right. Don't worry."

Dean turned, drying his face on a dish towel. "Shut up, Pig. Sit down."

I sat down. Dean lit a cigarette and blew smoke from the side of his mouth. Trying to look tough. What he looked like was a dork.

"I want the money," he said.

I looked into his eyes, waiting for him to go on. He looked back. I looked at Alex. Alex sniffed. I looked at Dean.

"I want the money," he repeated. "The sixty thousand."

"I haven't got it," I said.

He curled his lip. "Listen, Pig, it's simple. You give me the money, I give you the tape. If you don't give me the money, I give the tape to the police. Understand?"

"I understand. But I haven't got the money."

"Don't give me that crap," he sneered, taking the tape recorder from his pocket. He wound it forward again, then pressed Play. My tinny voice came on in mid-sentence.

". . . sixty thousand bucks. I'm rich. I'll buy you a new car."

"But the money's in the bank, in your dad's account."

"I've got his checkbook and bank card. . . . I'm sure we can work something out."

"I hope you know what you're doing."

Click.

A smug grin creased Dean's face.

"All right," I admitted. "But I can't withdraw the whole lot, can I? I can't get —"

"That's your problem," he said.

"How am I supposed to —"

"You're not listening, Pig. I want the money. I don't care how you get it." He flipped out the mini-cassette. "See this?"

I nodded.

"Alex?"

Alex sniffed tearfully and looked at him.

"This," he went on, waving the cassette in his hand, "this will put you both away. This will ruin your lives. It's yours for sixty thousand dollars."

"When?" I said.

"When what?"

"When do you want the money?"

The question surprised him. To tell you the truth, it surprised me. A part of me felt as if I didn't know what I was doing, but another part — deep within me — was thinking things through. I was a passenger in my own mind. Passenger, driver. *It's all right,* the driver was saying, *just leave it to me. I know what I'm doing. Look at him.* I looked at Dean. *See? He hasn't got a clue.*

It was true. Dean was fiddling nervously with his ponytail, swishing it all over the place, trying to think of what to say. Loose strands of lank blond hair floated to the floor.

"Monday," he said, eventually. "Noon, Monday."

"OK," I said.

Dean and Alex both stared at me.

"But —" began Alex.

"It's all right," I said.

"OK then," said Dean.

"OK," I said.

"Monday."

"Monday."

"Noon."

"Noon."

"Right. I'll be here, Monday, at noon."

I nodded.

"You'd better have the money."

I nodded again.

"OK then." He dropped his cigarette to the floor and stepped on it, then picked up his helmet and headed for the door. I glanced at the flattened cigarette. It was disgusting. He was disgusting.

"Dean?" I said.

He turned. "What?"

"How many copies of the tape are there?"

He paused. "What?"

"You've made copies of the tape?"

"I'm not stupid."

"No." I watched his eyes. "You wouldn't come here, on your own, with the only copy, would you? That *would* be stupid."

His mouth twitched as he tried to laugh. "I've got copies, don't worry about that."

I looked out of the window. It was quiet and empty outside, nothing moved. I glanced at the utensil jar by the stove — wooden spoons, potato masher, roasting fork, carving knives. I felt Alex's eyes watching me. We looked at each other. I saw uncertainty in her face. Fear, perhaps. Or was it something else? Understanding? A silent suggestion?

I turned to Dean. "I want all the copies."

"When I get the money, you'll get the tapes."

"How will I know?"

"What?"

"How will I know you haven't kept a copy?"

"You'll just have to trust me," he smirked.

I stared at the floor. I stared at the dead filaments of hair littering the clean linoleum. My mind was remarkably clear. I could see all the possibilities, I understood the probabilities, I'd calculated the odds. I felt alive, as if this was something I was born to.

I raised my eyes. "See you later, Dean."

He hesitated, trying to think of something clever to say, but nothing came to him. So he just sniffed a couple of times, flicked his ponytail again, and then left. I looked across at Alex and smiled and together we listened to the irritating buzz of his motorcycle as it started up and raced away. We listened until the sound had disappeared into the night.

"Bastard," Alex whispered.

"True," I replied.

"I'm sorry, Martyn."

"It's not your fault."

"I knew what he was like."

"Well . . ."

She half-smiled. "You told me so."

"It doesn't matter."

She stood up, ran her fingers through her hair, then sat down again. "What are we going to do now? It won't work. Your plan won't work anymore. We can't get rid of the body then pretend we don't know anything about it when it's found. Not now that Dean knows. It won't work. What are we going to do?"

I made some tea, and then I told her what we were going to do.

Later, after Alex had left, I went back into the kitchen with a pair of tweezers and carefully collected the loose hairs that had fallen from Dean's head and placed them in an envelope. Then I looked for the cigarette he'd extinguished on the floor and found it squashed beside the chair leg and I placed that in the envelope, too.

Usually, I think a lot in bed. Just before dropping off to sleep, when the silence and darkness of the night are absolute, that's when I think best. No noise, nothing to look at, no distractions, just pure thought. But that night, even though there were a thousand things to think about, I was asleep within minutes. A lovely, quiet drifting away into the oblivion of sleep. A journey into nothing. The demons I'd invited into my head the night before were gone. There was nothing there to bother me. Nothing.

I slept a long and dreamless sleep.

FRIDAY

"I don't like it, Martyn."

It was eleven o'clock in the morning. Alex and I were standing over Dad's body, the sheet removed. His staring eyes were nothing like eyes.

"It's nothing to be scared of," I said. "Just imagine he's asleep."

"Not dead, just sleeping."

"What?"

"That's what it says on gravestones — not dead, just sleeping."

"A dirty trick," I said.

She laughed nervously.

I stooped down and took the body under the arms, testing the weight. It was heavy. Very heavy. "I'll take this end," I said. "You take his feet."

Alex just stood there, wiping her hands on the back of her jeans.

I looked up at her. "The sooner we do it, the sooner it's over."

She was breathing heavily. I waited. She rubbed the back of her neck, looked to one side, wiped her hands once more, then took a deep breath and crouched down.

"This might take some time," I said.

And it did.

Dad wasn't that tall, and apart from his beer belly and his overall flabbiness, he wasn't really that fat, either. But now that he was dead he weighed a ton, and it took us the best part of an hour to get him up the stairs. He was a bit stiff as well, and his arms and legs kept getting caught in the banisters, which didn't help. But we got there in the end. We carried, we dragged, we pushed, we shoved, until eventually we got him into his bedroom and laid him out on the bed.

"Tea?" I suggested, rubbing the small of my back.

Alex said nothing, just nodded, out of breath.

The view from the kitchen window hadn't changed. Gray skies hanging over the tops of houses. Dull triangles decorated with dead chimney pots and television aerials. Right angles. Broken gutters. Ugly white satellite dishes.

"Martyn?"

I watched the curved black trace of a crow as it arced across the morning sky.

"Martyn?"

"What?"

"Are we bad?"

I swallowed a mouthful of tea. Alex was idly tracing a finger around the rim of her mug.

"Depends what you mean by bad," I answered.

"Bad. Evil. Wrong."

"Maybe. I don't know. It's a relative kind of thing, badness."

"How's that?"

"Good, bad. Right, wrong. What's the difference? Who decides?"

"But what we're doing — it's against the law."

I shrugged. "What's the law? It's only someone's opinion."

She was quiet for a while. I watched a starling alight on the window ledge and scrape its beak against the wood. Beady eyes stared back at me, black and shiny. Then it cocked its head and flew off.

"But," Alex went on, "surely *some* things are wrong. You know, just *wrong*. Universally wrong."

"Like what?"

"I don't know . . . murder, rape, stuff like that."

"Whatever anyone does, it's not wrong to them. Otherwise they wouldn't do it, would they?"

"No, but . . ."

"It's only wrong if you think it's wrong. If you think it's right, and others think it's wrong, then it's only wrong if you get caught."

She frowned. "Is that what you really think?"

I sighed. "I don't know. Maybe. Maybe not. I'm just thinking out loud."

She shook her head. "Yeah, well . . . let's just hope that God doesn't exist."

"Why?"

"He'd never forgive us for what we're about to do."

"He would if he knew why."

We talked on for a while longer, just passing the time, avoiding reality, delaying what we both knew had to be done. Her mom had got an audition, she told me. Goneril in *King Lear*, a regional theater production. . . . Is that good? . . . Better than nothing. . . . Did you see that program about cuttlefish? . . . That's a nice bag. Is it new? . . . Do you want anything to eat? . . .

But eventually the subject turned back to the business at hand.

"Mom's getting the car back today," Alex said.

"Can you get it for tonight?"

"Not without her knowing. She's staying in."

"What about tomorrow?"

"She's working in the afternoon but I think she's going out later on. A friend's party. She'll be drinking, so she won't take the car."

"How late will she get back?"

"Late."

"We'll have to do it Saturday night, then."

"I suppose."

We sat in silence for a while.

That was one of the things I liked about Alex. She understood that you don't have to talk all the time, that it's all right just to sit there, nice and quiet, thinking together. Most people, they just keep yapping all the time, even when there's nothing to say. Talking for the sake of it, spouting garbage. Making noise. What's wrong with silence? Listen to it, it's beautiful.

Somewhere up the street a car started up, music booming from the stereo. *D-doomp-d-doomp-doomp tss tss tss tss d-doomp-d-doomp-doomp*.

Not so beautiful.

I wondered what Alex was thinking about. Me? Perhaps she

was wondering what I was thinking about. Who knows what someone else is thinking? You can't even be sure that anyone else is thinking at all. How do you know? You don't. You'll never know. All you can do is assume that what's in your head is the same sort of stuff that's in everyone else's. You don't even know for sure that anything else is real. How do you know? It could all be a dream. I've even thought sometimes that maybe I'm the *only* thing that exists. Maybe everything else is just there for me. Everything and everybody. All made up, just for me. And when I'm not there, it all just fades away.

Alex sighed quietly.

"Right," I said, glancing at the clock. "Aunty Jean's due at four. We'd better get moving."

I removed Dad's jacket, shirt, shoes, and socks, pulled up the duvet so it half-covered his head, then stepped back to take a look. The wound over his eye looked odd — colorless, cold, deep.

"Alex, did you bring — What are you doing?"

She turned from the open wardrobe. "Nothing. I was just putting his clothes away." Dad's shoes dangled from her hand.

"Just leave them," I said, looking around. "The messier it is the more natural it'll look. I'll have to dress him again, anyway."

She grinned awkwardly, shut the wardrobe door, and dumped the shoes on the floor.

"Did you bring those bandages?" I asked her.

She dipped into her bag and handed me a bandage. I peeled off the backing and placed it over the cut on Dad's head.

"How's that?"

"Looks all right," Alex replied. There was an edge to her voice. She was tense and fidgety, eyes darting all over the room. It was hardly surprising, really. I felt kind of edgy myself.

"Are you ready?" I asked her.

For a second I thought she was going to chicken out. But then she nodded grimly and delved into her bag again. It was a big old duffel bag with pockets and zippers all over the place, big enough to carry a small horse. After rummaging around inside it for a minute she stepped forward carrying a makeup bag.

"Not too much," I reminded her. "Just enough to, you know, give him a bit of life."

She opened the makeup bag and took out a small plastic case, flipped it open, and loaded a floppy little brush with pinkish powder. A lick of her lips. A quick, nervous glance at me. A deep breath. And then, muttering something to herself, she bent over the bed and went to work.

I watched her as she applied the blusher to the deathly gray face. Her hands were shaking. I didn't have to see her face to know she'd have that faraway look of concentration in her eyes, her tongue poking out from the corner of her mouth, little wrinkles on her brow. Just how she looked when we played Scrabble. I couldn't help smiling to myself. Look at her, I thought. Getting tall now, taller than me. And, you know, kind of curvy. Just look at her. In her extra-large lumberjack shirt and faded black jeans, her funny little pink canvas shoes, her slim, ringed fingers and ears dotted with tiny black studs. Look at that girl. Who else would do that for you? Who else?

My heart sang.

What a ridiculous thing to be doing, I thought, painting the face of your father. It's like playing with dolls. Playing make-believe. Like the games I used to play when I was a kid. In my room, on my own, making things up. Martyn the Cowboy, drifting aimlessly across the plains. Just me and my horse, riding through the badlands, sleeping beneath the trail of stars. Martyn the Avenger, feared throughout the kingdom. Wrongs righted and villainy vanquished. Martyn the Assassin, cold-eyed and calculating, a hunter. A killer. I don't remember *doing* anything, I just imagined things. Fights, quests, journeys. I could go anywhere. Imaginary worlds, a universe of my own. A place where nothing mattered because nothing was real.

I don't know when all that stopped. You reach a certain age when reality grabs you by the scruff of the neck and shouts in your face: "Hey, look, *this* is what life is." And you have to open your eyes and look at it, listen to it, smell it: people who don't like you, things you don't want to do, things that hurt, things that scare you, questions without answers, feelings you don't understand, feelings you don't want but have no control over.

Reality.

When you gradually come to realize all that stuff in books, films, television, magazines, newspapers, comics — it's all garbage. It's got nothing to do with anything. It's all made up. It doesn't happen like that. It's not real. It means nothing. Reality is what you see when you look out of the window of a bus: dour faces, sad and temporary lives, millions of cars, metal, bricks, glass, rain, cruel laughter, ugliness, dirt, bad teeth, crippled pigeons, little kids in strollers who've already forgotten how to smile. . . .

"Martyn?"

Alex had stepped away from the bed. She looked pale. I went over and examined Dad's face. He looked ill, but not dead.

"Excellent," I said.

"You'll have to close his eyes."

I'd seen it done in films. You spread your hand and — with your thumb and middle finger extended — gently close the eyelids. I leaned over the bed.

"They won't stay closed."

"What?"

I tried again, using two hands, but when I let go, Dad's eyelids slowly yawned back open. "They won't close."

"Why not?"

"I don't know."

Alex peered over my shoulder. I could feel the heat of her breath on my neck. I looked around and pointed to a pair of pants on the floor. "Pass me those."

Alex reached down and passed me the pants. I shook them and heard coins rattle, felt in the pocket, and pulled out two coins.

One on each eye.

"That's better."

"Don't forget to take them off when your aunty gets here."

I grinned.

She almost grinned back. I stepped away from the bed and took another look.

"What do you think?"

"He certainly looks ill."

"Do you think she'll notice he's not breathing?"

Alex wrinkled her nose. "I don't know about that, but unless she's lost her sense of smell she's bound to notice that stink."

I went to the bathroom and fetched a load of medicine stuff from the cabinet — aspirins, Night Nurse, VapoRub, tissues,

Theraflu. When I came back, Alex was standing over by the dresser.

"Are you all right?" I asked her.

She nodded. "Just a bit queasy."

I piled all the medicine stuff on the bedside table then smeared a ton of VapoRub all over the place; on the duvet, on the pillow, around Dad's neck. The pungent fumes wafted in the air, disguising the sweet, musty smell of death. I was still bothered about the lack of breathing.

"What's the time?"

Alex looked at her watch. "Three o'clock."

"We could make a tape," I suggested.

"What?"

"Just a minute." I went to my room and came back with my cassette recorder and the little microphone that came with it. "Snoring sounds, breathing," I explained, sticking a blank tape in and holding out the mike. "You can do it, Alex."

"I've never heard him *sleeping*," she said. "I can't imitate what I don't know."

So I showed her. I snorted, snored, breathed heavily, mumbled. "Like that," I said, "only in Dad's voice."

We practiced for a while. She got it almost right away.

"What do you think?" she asked.

I nodded, smiling. "Perfect." I held out the mike. "Ready?"

She breathed in and nodded, and I pressed RECORD.

Five minutes later we had what we needed. The sound of a sleeping, snoring, snuffling Dad. Alex even added an incoherent mumble here and there for extra authenticity.

When I put the tape recorder under the duvet and played it back it sounded even better — muffled, realistic.

"First take, too," I said. "You've got this acting business sorted."

"That's not acting," she said, panting slightly, "that's just breathing."

Dad's bedroom had always been pretty grungy. Smelly, dirty, kind of sticky everywhere. A bit spooky, too. It was like a cave, a secret hideaway, a grotto. Even on a sunny day it was cold and dark. Now, though, with Dad's body laid out in disguise — perfumed, made-up, artificial — and the afternoon light filtering in through closed curtains, it was an incredibly eerie place to be. Chilling, macabre, like something that belonged in a different world.

"Come on," I said. "Let's get out of here."

At the door I turned and looked back. There he was. Not dead, just sleeping.

It would have to do.

My room was like a palace compared to Dad's. Clean and white and odorless. Everything in its place. It was three-thirty. Just enough time for a quick rest before Aunty Jean showed up. I breathed in and relaxed.

"How do you feel?" I asked Alex.

"Not too good, actually," she said, rummaging through her bag. "In fact . . . I feel a bit ill. I think . . ." She put the bag down and put a hand to her stomach.

"Are you going to be sick?"

She looked at me, nodding her head.

"All right," I said, going over to her. "It'll be all right. Use the bathroom. Come on." As I led her out of the bedroom she started gulping, holding her hand to her mouth.

"I'm sorry," she said. "I thought . . . uh. . . ."

"Don't worry about it."

"It's embarrassing. . . ."

"It doesn't matter."

"But I don't want to . . . uh . . . it's so embarrassing . . . being sick. . . . Would you mind going downstairs? . . . I don't want you to hear me . . . you know. . . ."

"That's OK. You can shut the door. Lock it if you want. I'll be in the front room. Don't worry, I won't hear anything."

I got her into the bathroom, shut the door, and went downstairs. In the front room I opened the curtains and smiled as the sunlight crept in for the first time since . . . since when? Since Wednesday. Two days ago. I swept the fireplace, wiped it down with a damp cloth, dried it, then gave it a thorough polishing. The smell of "Autumn Flowers" filled the room, almost hiding that other smell. Almost, but not quite. Cigarettes, I thought. That would help, the smell of cigarettes. I found a pack on the mantelpiece, took one out, lit it, and placed it in an ashtray, letting it burn. I sniffed in deeply — not bad. Maybe it would be all right.

Shuffling sounds from upstairs. Taps running. The roar of the toilet flushing. Alex. Being sick.

I crossed to the window and looked out. The same old gray day looked back at me. A fat Jack Russell terrier padded across the road and peed on the back wheel of a white Fiesta, then ambled away. A couple of minutes later Slobman from up the road slouched past the window, mindless indifference hanging from his face. Where was he going? I wondered. Nowhere, probably. He never went anywhere. He just slobbed around. He was ageless. Sometimes he looked like a young man, sometimes he looked fifty. With his ratty old coat hanging open, his Garfield T-shirt tucked into army surplus jogging pants, and his wispy hair waving in the wind, he turned the corner and was gone.

Main road traffic droned in the distance, humming, whooshing, moving. Always moving. Cars, people in cars, going places. But the street outside was still. My street. It branches off the main road, loops around, then rejoins the main road again at the bottom. Like the curved part of a letter D, the straight part being the main road. That's why it's relatively quiet here: The street doesn't go anywhere.

The clock was ticking. Quarter to four. Come on, Alex, I thought. Hurry up. Aunty Jean will be here soon. The toilet flushed again. A door closed. I listened for the sound of footsteps on the stairs — nothing. Come *on*.

I stared out at the mid-afternoon emptiness. Terraced houses with faded doors and faded curtains, alleyways, low brick walls and chipped pillars, paint-peeled gates, raggedy hedges — the look of deadness in the air like nothing-ever-happens. I knew it so well it didn't look like anything.

Ten to four. The toilet flushed again.

I went over and sat down in the armchair. The armchair. Dad's armchair. *My* armchair.

Footsteps creaked on the ceiling. I looked up. What is she *doing*?

Come on, Alex.

Come *on*.

At five minutes to four I couldn't wait any longer. I went to the foot of the stairs and looked up. The bathroom door was still closed. "Alex?"

No answer.

"Alex! Come on, she'll be here —"

The door opened and Alex popped her head out — head and bare shoulders. "Sorry," she said. "I won't be a minute. I got sick on my shirt, I was just wiping it off."

I didn't know where to look. "Oh . . . right . . . OK. It's just that . . . you know. . . ."

"I won't be a sec —"

And then the doorbell rang.

I could tell it was Aunty Jean by the tone of the bell. It sounded terrified. I glanced quickly at the door, then looked up at Alex. Despite the sudden race of panic I couldn't help noticing how different she looked. There was nothing . . . you know . . . nothing *improper* about it. Just a hint of bare shoulder and one bare arm. But somehow it made her look so graceful, like an actress. Like a film star dressing for her big scene.

"Martyn!" she hissed.

"Stay there!" I hissed back. "Keep the door shut and don't make a sound. I'll try and get rid of her as quick as I can."

The bell was ringing again, demanding to be answered. I waited for Alex to shut the door, took a couple of deep breaths, then went and opened the front door. And there she was — Aunty Jean. Stiff, upright, scowling, standing on the step as if she'd been waiting there for a thousand years.

"Well?" she said.

Pale winter sunlight had broken through the patchy clouds, glistening weakly on the roofs of parked cars across the street. Aunty Jean's pancaked face soaked up the sun like blotting paper.

I stepped back and motioned her in with a nervous smile. "Thank *you*," she said.

Her shiny brown coat rustled as she entered the hall. She was a ludicrous person. Bony, leathery, with sticky-out elbows and bowlegs, she looked like a cartoon woman. A crazy old spook.

She removed her coat and passed it to me without looking.

"Dad's sick, Aunty," I said, hanging up her coat. "He's in bed."

"Sick?" she snorted. "So that's what he calls it now, is it?"

She looped the strap of her handbag over her shoulder and adjusted the hang of her dress. It was the same dress she always wore, a stiff cream-colored thing with shiny brass buttons. Stiff enough to stand up on its own.

"No, he really is *sick*," I said. "Flu or something, a virus."

She snorted again. A phlegmy, back-of-the-throat noise, complete with flared nostrils and a curled upper lip. Her teeth were remarkably small, like baby's teeth. Small and square. I'd often wondered if they were false. She marched into the front room and I followed her, like some kind of weird offspring following its mother.

"*Whooof*," she exclaimed. "What on *earth* is that smell?"

"Drains," I spluttered, "the drains up the road are being fixed."

"I didn't see anything."

"No, they *were* being fixed, a couple of days ago. They were digging up the road. They didn't fix them properly."

"Hmmm," she said.

Then she was pacing around the room, looking into every corner, checking for dust, beer cans, bottles. I stood there watching her, hoping she was as mad as she looked. Her hair sat on top of her head like a blue Brillo pad, rigid and unmoving. Why does she do that to it? I thought. Does she think it looks nice? What does it *feel* like? A nylon brush? A hedgehog?

"How's school?" she said.

"What?"

"Don't say *what*, say *pardon*."

"Pardon?"

"School, Martyn. How are you doing at school?"

"OK," I shrugged.

"OK? What's that supposed to mean?"

I rubbed at the back of my neck. "Everything's fine, Aunty. Thank you."

She came toward me and stopped about an inch away, staring into my eyes. She smelled of lemon and bleach and awful old-woman perfume.

"Now then, Martyn," she said in her very serious voice, "I want you to tell me the truth."

I stared back into her face, avoiding her eyes. A long black hair twisted from a mole on her chin. The pores of her skin were stained, like small blue stars.

"How *are* you?" she breathed. "*Really*."

I licked my lips and tried to swallow. "Fine, Aunty. Really. I'm fine."

"What about *him*?"

She said *him* as if it were the vilest word in the English language.

"He's OK. . . . He's doing his best. Really. It's all right, we're all right."

She gazed deeper into my eyes, trying to read my mind, then turned away and said something that sounded suspiciously like *hmph!*

"Where is he then?" she said dismissively, "Where's the *patient*?"

As I led her up the stairs my heart was pounding and my stomach felt like it was full of wasps. She kept sniffing all the time, not saying anything, just sniffing. Sniff, sniff, sniff. Like a labrador searching for a bone. I couldn't help glancing at the bathroom door as we passed, imagining Alex in there, imagining. . . .

We stopped outside Dad's bedroom. "He's probably still asleep," I said. "He was up most of the night."

Aunty Jean rolled her eyes.

"I mean he didn't get any sleep," I explained. "He was up, you know, getting sick all the time, in and out of bed."

She gave me a skeptical look. "Open the door, then."

There are moments in your life when you have to do things you really don't want to do. You *have* to do them, you have no choice. It's no good wishing things were different, wishing you could turn back the clock, wishing you had another chance, because things aren't different, you can't turn back the clock, you don't get another chance. So, there I was, about to present Aunty Jean to her dead brother, hoping I could get away with pretending that he was ill in bed, asleep. Not dead, just sleeping.

I had no choice. Do you understand? I had *no choice*.

The only thing to do when you're faced with something like that is to say to yourself: What's the worst that can happen? And then do it.

I opened the door and we went in.

"*Phewf!* There's that smell again. Goodness me!"

I ignored her and moved cautiously into the dim and fetid room. "Dad?" I whispered. "Dad? It's Aunty Jean."

"Why is it so dark in here?" she moaned. "I can't see where I'm going."

"The light hurts his eyes," I explained as I hurriedly removed the coins from Dad's eyelids. I'd forgotten all about them. Luckily, his eyes stayed shut. I reached under the covers and switched on the tape recorder. Muffled heavy breathing growled from beneath the sheets. Snores. Too loud. I fumbled for the volume control and turned it down.

Aunty Jean was standing in the middle of the room tutting. "Look at the state of this place, look at it, it's *disgusting*."

I reached my hand in under Dad's head, shuddering. It was cold, lifeless.

"He's fast asleep, Aunty," I said.

"Is he, now?"

She approached the bed with some menace. Rasping snores filled the room. Had we overdone it? I moved Dad's head in time with the snoring.

Aunty Jean stopped a few feet away, a look of surprise on her face.

"Oh," she said.

She bent forward for a closer look. I held my breath.

"He's a bit . . . off-color."

"He hasn't been eating much," I said.

"What happened to his head?"

"He walked into the door during the night. Got a nasty cut." She stepped closer, sniffing. "What *is* that smell?"

"He's had a bit of . . . you know, a bit of stomach trouble."

I was starting to worry if we'd recorded enough snoring on the tape. What was I going to do if the tape ran out?

My heart raced as Aunty Jean moved a little closer.

"*Will*-yam? *Will*-yam?" She reached out her hand.

"Better not, Aunty," I said. "It might be contagious."

She snapped her hand away.

A puzzled look wrinkled her features. "He looks . . . he certainly doesn't look well, Martyn. Have you called the doctor?"

I almost laughed out loud. "Tomorrow," I said. "The doctor's coming tomorrow."

"His eyes . . . there's something strange about his eyes," she said, squinting in the dark. "Perhaps I ought to call the doctor now."

"No, no, really. I . . . I called the doctor earlier. They said it was probably this virus that's going around. It makes your eyes look funny, apparently."

"Hmmm," she said.

The tape recorder was beginning to slow down — the batteries must have been worn out. The snores were getting slower and slower and the tape mechanism was starting to whine laboriously.

"What's that noise?"

"Pipes," I said. "There's something wrong with the plumbing."

"Drains, pipes, what else doesn't work in this house?"

The tape was really struggling, now. It sounded like the dying groans of a sea monster.

"I think we ought to go now," I suggested. "Let him sleep." As I moved from the bed, removing my hand from Dad's neck, his head lolled back and clonked against the headboard.

"What was *that*?" asked Aunty Jean.

"Nothing. Come on," I said, ushering her out. "I'll make us some tea."

"Your hands smell," she commented as I led her to the door.

"VapoRub," I explained, breathing a silent sigh of relief as I closed the bedroom door.

I'd made some tea and opened up a packet of cookies and there we were, aunt and nephew, sitting in the kitchen, munching, sipping, and talking. At least, Aunty Jean was talking. I was just munching and sipping and staring at the table.

". . . and, of course, when he was your age, your father was *always* getting into trouble — playing hooky, stealing, smoking, drinking. Oh, yes, he was drinking even then — cider, sherry, whatever he could get his hands on. Made life miserable for our poor mother, I can tell you. Miserable. It's no wonder she couldn't cope. Father, I mean, your grandpa, God rest his soul, he tried his best. Discipline, that's what he used to say, discipline, that boy needs plenty of discipline. And he got it, too. Father beat him within an inch of his life sometimes, but he still never learned. Never had any respect, that was his trouble, never learned respect for his elders. Why can't you be more like your sister? they used to tell him. Like apples and oranges, we were, apples and oranges. I don't know. He was an embarrassment, that's what he was, an embarrassment to the family. I remember once . . ."

As she jabbered on I wondered if she'd still be talking like this if she knew he was dead. Jabber, jabber, jabber . . . just look at her, her mouth never stops moving. What a sight. Ha, she's got cookie crumbs stuck on her lip. Yakkety yakkety yak. Your father this, your father that. On and on. How many times have

I heard all this? How can she blame him, anyway? None of us has any control over what we do. If you're good, you're good — if you're bad, you're bad. That's all there is to it. You can't change the way you're made. And even if you could, it wouldn't be down to you. It's your genes. It's all in your genes, your DNA. Asking someone to change how they are is like asking a rock to change color — it can't be done. Simple as that. You don't blame a rock for being rock-colored, do you? You don't say — come on now, rock, you can do better than that, you can be bright blue if you try. No, you are what you are and there's nothing anyone can do about it. I mean, take Aunty Jean, for example. It's not her fault she's a blue-haired, bowlegged dragon lady. She can't help it. Of course, that doesn't mean I have to *like* her, but I have no right to judge her, either. In the same way I have no right to judge anything — a fly, a rat, a tapeworm, whatever. You can hardly blame a fly for being a dirty little buzzy thing, can you? That's just what it is, it didn't make a choice. No one said to it, What do you want to be? A pony? A flower? A nun? Or how about a dirty little fly? It had no options. Just as we have no options. You get what you're given. Like it or lump it.

"... ruined your poor mother's life and he's going to ruin yours, too, if you're not careful. Martyn? *Martyn?* Are you listening?"

"Yes, Aunty, I'm listening. More tea?"

She glanced at the clock. "Goodness, is that the time? I have to be going." She rose from the table, brushing at the steellike folds in her dress.

"I'll get your coat," I said.

"Just a moment, I have to use the facilities."

"Wha — Pardon?"

"The lady's facilities."

The bathroom.

"The . . . uh . . . the facilities are out of order, Aunty."

"Don't be ridiculous."

"It's the plumbing."

She just snorted at me and marched off toward the stairs. I chased after her. "Aunty! No, you can't. It doesn't work. Honest. The water tank is broken." But she was already halfway up the stairs; she wasn't going to stop. All I could do was try and warn Alex. "You can't use the *bathroom*, Aunty!" I yelled. "You can't go in the *BATHROOM*!"

At the top of the stairs she turned and looked down at me as if I was crazy. I didn't know what to do, so I just grinned like an idiot and shrugged. She shook her head, then opened the bathroom door.

What could I do?

I held my breath and waited for the scream. My heart was thumping like a bass drum — *d-dum, d-dum, d-dum*. One second, five seconds, ten seconds . . . nothing. I started breathing again. After a minute or two I heard the sound of flushing, followed by taps running. Then the bathroom door opened and Aunty Jean came out clutching her handbag. She looked down at me. I was standing rigidly at the bottom of the stairs, gripping the banister in both hands, staring up at her with wide-open eyes.

"What *are* you doing?" she said.

"Nothing," I said, relieved. "I'll get your coat."

"What was all that nonsense about?" she said as she started down the stairs. "Plumbing? Broken water tank? There's nothing wrong with it at all."

"I forgot," I said. "It was fixed. The plumber came around when I wasn't here. Here's your coat."

She turned to let me help her on with her coat. "I'm worried about you, Martyn. Seriously. You're getting as bad as your father. Your memory is hopeless. It's no wonder your schoolwork is suffering."

Schoolwork suffering? "I'm just a bit tired, Aunty. Looking after Dad while he's ill, you know. . . ."

"You want to get this house looked at," she said, hitching up her coat. "It stinks in here."

"I'll give it a good cleaning," I said.

"Yes, well . . . it's not just the house that needs a good cleaning."

I opened the front door. "Thanks for coming, Aunty. I'll tell Dad you were here; he'll be sorry he missed you."

"I bet he will," she said.

I leaned out and looked up at the sky. "Looks like rain, again."

"Hmmm," she answered, pulling on a pair of white gloves and stepping out into the street. "I'll be back soon. You tell your father, I'll be back soon."

"I'll tell him, Aunty. Have a safe trip home."

She didn't say good-bye, thanks for the tea, or anything, just marched off down the street, her sensible shoes clumping on the pavement. I watched her turn the corner at the bottom of the road, watched a little more to make sure she wasn't coming back, then I shut the door and sank to the floor with a huge sigh. I felt drained.

"Has she gone?"

Alex was standing at the top of the stairs, fully dressed.

"She's gone," I said.

"That was close."

"Where *were* you?"

"In the bathroom."

I got to my feet. "I know *that*. Why didn't she see you?"

"I guessed she had to go to the bathroom so I hid behind the shower curtain."

I smiled. "Good thinking."

"I'm not just a pretty face, you know."

That was true.

"I nearly gave myself away, though," she said. "You should have heard the noises she was making, like a balloon deflating." We both giggled as she imitated the sound of Aunty Jean farting. "I had to stuff a towel in my mouth to stop myself from laughing. I thought I was going to die."

"I'll mention it next time I see her," I promised. "Are you all right now? You look a lot better."

Alex hooked her bag over her shoulder and came downstairs. "Yeah, I'm fine. Sorry about that."

"No problem."

"No." She smiled. "It was close, though, wasn't it?"

"Close enough."

"What would she have done if she'd seen me?"

"Exploded, probably."

Early evening. Alex had gone home. I was alone in my bedroom. I lay on the bed and closed my eyes, trying to rest, but I couldn't. There was too much stuff racing around in my head.

I got up and crossed to the window. The winter-black night was still. Arrows of orange light lasered out from the streetlights illuminating the dim surroundings of my world. Parked cars, cracked pavement decorated with cakes of curled-up dog mess, lanky urban weeds sprouting from the crumbled gaps in a dirty brick wall. The weeds were colorless in the dark.

Where does the color go?

In the distance I could see imperfect rows of a thousand other houses, all the same. Pale yellow lights winking in the windows. In every house, I realized, there'd be a story of some kind: a family drama, a tragedy, a love story, a comedy. Right now, scenes were being acted out, plots followed, stories told. Fights, arguments, sex, betrayal, revenge, boredom, cunning, evil, bad luck, laughter, desire, delight, death . . .

What did I care? None of it had anything to do with me.

In the street below, two shaven-headed kids were swaggering down the road swigging from cans of beer. Their raised voices echoed in the backstreet silence, a hooded, primitive sound: *aingonnatellya . . . I tellya . . . 'e'sadeadmaninnit . . .* Vacant animal eyes, looking for something, anything, nothing. One of them spat through his teeth as they passed beneath the window, then they were gone.

Alcohol. It sucks the life out of a face and replaces it with its own dumb shine of inanity. It's up to you. If you want to lose yourself, have a drink.

Look at this place. These squalid houses, dirty little streets, dead skies. Nothing. No life, no point. Too many people with nothing to say and nothing to do and nowhere to go. Gray souls. Waiting for it all to end. This is it, this is what I have. This. This place where tiny things mean so much to tiny people. Where nobody does anything, where we eat, drink, breed, age, and die. This is it. A new millennium. The Age of

Technology. The end result of millions of years of evolution. Me, alone in a dirty little house, in a dirty little street, in a dirty little town.

I closed the curtains, turned off the bedroom light, and lay down in the dark.

I thought of Alex and I thought of Dean and I thought of sixty thousand dollars. It was my money. It was my inheritance. My right. Mine. No one else was going to have it. I still hadn't figured out exactly how I was going to get it, or what I was going to do with it, but I was working on it. According to Alex, the check wouldn't clear until Tuesday. Using the bank card I could take out five hundred each day. Sixty thousand divided by five hundred is . . . a lot of days. How many days did I have? How many weeks? What would happen if . . . ? Too many questions. Think of something else. I thought of all the things we could do, me and Alex. Young and rich. Free. We could go anywhere, do anything. I could set up my own private detective agency — me and Alex, gumshoes, private eyes. We could rent one of those run-down offices in a shady part of town, with my own desk, filing cabinets for my files, one of those big slow fans on the ceiling, venetian blinds, a waiting room for clients, the smoked-glass door panel lettered in flaking black paint: *Martyn Pig — Investigations*. That'd be all right. Alex could drive me around, I'd buy her a sports car . . . or I could buy a small island. Right out in the middle of the sea where no one else could get to. We could live there, make friends with the animals, build a little cabin, spend all day talking, walking on the beach. And at nighttime we'd light a fire and watch the sun go down over the sea and listen to the sound of waves breaking gently on the shore. . . . Or we could go to Australia, or America, find some remote place out in the desert where Indians used to live. The badlands, miles and miles of nothing. Hot, dry wasteland, shifting sands, towering red mountains, canyons, ghost towns. We could ride horses. . . .

I drifted into a shallow sleep and my thoughts shimmied into fragile dreams. Scraps of images fluttered in my mind: Dad, Mom, Alex, Dean, Morse, Holmes, Aunty Jean, detectives, islands, deserts, horses . . . all floating around in meaningless circles. As I half-slept in the curtained darkness, stray sounds from the street outside darted in and out of my semiconsciousness, merging with the disjointed thoughts, weaving reality into dreams.

When I woke my mouth was dry and my eyes were sticky with sleep. It was nine o'clock in the evening. I was still tired.

I didn't know what to do.

For the moment, there was nothing more to think about. All I had to do was wait.

I went to the bathroom. I washed my hands, washed my face. I brushed my teeth, trying to get rid of that furry feeling in my mouth. I changed clothes, put on a clean T-shirt, clean underwear, clean jeans. I went downstairs and made a cheese sandwich and a cup of tea. I watched television. A cop show, I don't know what it's called. That man from *Miami Vice* was in it, the blond one, cracking jokes and chasing crooks down alleys with a big gun in his hand. That was all right. When it finished, I changed channels and watched some stand-up comedians swearing and telling rude jokes for half an hour. It wasn't funny. At eleven o'clock, I turned off the television and sat for a while in the dark listening to the sound of Friday night drunks going home — slurred shouts, cold laughter, cars revving, doors slamming. I sat there until the early hours of the morning when the silence was complete, and then I listened. I was listening for the hidden sounds that tell the story of this house. They must be there somewhere, in the walls, in the bricks, under the floor. Memories. But I didn't hear anything.

Two o'clock. I went into the kitchen and washed up my plate and cup, turned off the light, locked the doors, and went upstairs. Peed again, washed again, brushed my teeth again. Into the bedroom, undressed, got into bed, and fell asleep.

Another day gone.

SATURDAY

The morning arrived cold, dull, and heavy. I opened the bedroom curtains and gazed out at the colors of the day. Gray, brown. Brown, gray. Black. Dead green. The color had returned to the weeds on the wall. Dead green spikes drooped with the weight of frost.

A door slammed and the young couple from next door slouched out dragging their snotty-nosed kids across the street. The father flicked a dead cigarette into the gutter, adjusted the bright red Santa hat perched ridiculously on top of his head, and aimed his remote-control key at his car. Sidelights flashed and the alarm sounded — *weeweewee-weeweewee* — then stopped.

Why? Why does *everything* have to make a noise?

One of the kids was whining about something, tugging at his dad's belt. Dad didn't want to know.

"Get in the car and shut up," he grunted.

His wife coughed, stuck a cigarette in her mouth, got in the car, and slammed the door. The car roared into life and they raced away up the street.

Merry Christmas.

Downstairs, the sudden *pheep-pheep* of the telephone startled me. I swore, flicked hot tea from my sleeve, and picked up the phone.

"Hello?"

"Martyn?"

"Alex. You made me jump."

"What?"

"The phone ringing . . . it doesn't matter. What are you doing?"

"I have to go shopping."

"When?"

"Now. Mom's going to Sainsbury's. I have to help her with the shopping."

"Right."

She lowered her voice. "I think it's all right for later, you know. . . . "

"The car?"

"Yes."

"Good."

"Do you need anything?"

What kind of question is *that*? I thought to myself. Do I *need* anything? I need a million things. I need nothing.

"Like what?" I asked.

"Anything. Food, bread, milk, I don't know."

"No, I'm all right, thanks."

"OK." I heard her mom's voice in the background, telling her to hurry up. "Gotta go," she said. "I'll see you later."

The phone went dead.

I needed to get out of the house, that's what I needed. I needed to get some fresh air into my lungs, air that wasn't stained with the must of stale death.

The question was — where to go?

There's nowhere to go around here, nowhere that isn't full of noise and ugliness.

Where? Town, the park, the river?

The town would be jam-packed with Christmas shoppers, the park stinks . . . even the river's no good. A greasy brown stew lined with tough-looking fishermen in their army surplus rags, fishing idly, drinking beer, warning you off with get-away looks.

Where? There's got to be somewhere half-decent.

How about the beach?

The beach?

Why not? There'll be no one there, it'll be empty. Cold, big, wide open, and deserted . . .

Yes. The beach.

I started poking around the house looking for bus fare. A dollar here, fifty cents there. Then I remembered the money in Dad's room, the coins I'd placed on his eyes, and I grabbed those, too. The bedroom smelled really bad. Thick and gassy. Like sulfur. I covered my mouth and nose with a handkerchief and rummaged through Dad's pants pockets, coming up with another couple of bucks in change. More than enough. I pocketed it all, then got out of there before I was sick.

• • •

The beach is about twelve miles away, half an hour on the bus. It's actually an island. Just a small one. A mile or so long and half a mile wide. You wouldn't know it's an island, but it is. A long straight road takes you across great stretches of muddy ooze. The ooze is the estuary, so the road is really a bridge, but, like I say, you wouldn't know it. Except when there's a high tide and the ooze fills up with a dull-gray sea that laps slowly across the surface of the road and nothing can pass until the tide goes out again. Then you know it's an island.

Today, though, as the bus bumped along the bone-dry road, all I could see was miles and miles of sticky brown mud and waxy green grasses waving stiffly in the wind. I slid open the window and sniffed in the smell of the sea. Salty, fresh, clean.

The bus was almost empty. Just me and a funny-looking girl at the back reading a girls' magazine. She had too many teeth to fit her mouth and kept adjusting her lips to cover up her sticky-out teeth, like a fish sucking in water. *Gloop-gloop.* I watched her for a while, then got fed up with that and looked out of the window. We were on the island now. The bus was rattling along narrow roads lined with high hedges and wind-whipped trees, their branches occasionally scraping against the windows as the bus squeezed in tight to the side of the road. Behind the hedges lay dead-looking fields dotted with birds — seagulls, lapwings, rooks — pecking at the icy ground. Farmlands passed by in a blur of emptiness. Ramshackle buildings, tangled angles of weather-faded boards and rusted roof iron. Chicken wire, sheets of corrugated iron, a gutted tractor. Stables, too, half-acres of hard-packed ground laid out with strange patterns of colored show-jumping bars. Horse manure for sale in blue plastic sacks. False barns selling fruit and veg and false fresh eggs. Faded signs: PICK-YOUR-OWN, PALLETS FOR SALE, misspelled BABY RABITTS, BOXER PUPS, COCKATIELS. Pubs: The Dog and Pheasant, The Rose, Live and Let Live. Small rows of tiny cottages, hidden turnings, meaningless signs, churches in the middle of nowhere . . .

It felt strange being out of the house. Exciting, but a little scary, too. I wasn't used to it. My world consisted of my house, the street, school, and the occasional trip to town. Anywhere beyond that was an adventure. Pathetic, really. The exciting part about it was that no one knew where I was. No one. Not a soul. Apart from the bus driver and the fish-mouthed girl, of course. They knew *where* I was, but they didn't know *who* I was. I don't know why I found that exciting, but I did.

As we rounded another tight corner something glinted in the distance, a silver streak. I squinted through the smeared window but was unable to distinguish the sea from the sky. It was all just a blanket of aluminum gray.

The bus moved on into the heart of the island. Mud hollows, marshes full of wet brown reeds, more emptiness. Long-legged birds patrolled the mud banks, waders, sliding their long, curved beaks into the brown slime, looking for worms and mudgrubs. Grub. That's all they had to think about. Nothing else. Nothing to worry about but grub. Lucky birds.

Now I could see the sea. Far away, a thin sliver of shine at the end of the mud. A long black container ship was slinking across the horizon, low in the water, silent. Where was it from? I wondered. Where was it going? What was it carrying? Sugar? Grain? Molasses? What *are* molasses? Mole asses. Mole asses. A boat full of moles' asses.

The bus turned a corner and the sea view disappeared.

I sat back and closed my eyes. The first time I came here . . . when was the first time I came here? Years ago. With a friend, I think, someone from school. What was his name? I forget. He wasn't really a friend, just someone I hung around with for a while. I never liked him. He had a lazy eye, whatever that is. He wore glasses with a patch over one lens. Always had a stuffed-up nose. He spent the whole day going on about how *fandasdig* the beaches were in Greece, or Majorca, or somewhere. How *hod* it was, how clean it was, how *priddy* it was. . . .

Who cares?

After that I always came here on my own. And always in the winter, when it wasn't hot and it wasn't clean and it wasn't pretty.

One thing's for sure, I never came here with Dad. "Beach?" he'd say. "What d'ya wanna beach for?" Dad never went anywhere. We never went anywhere. Even before Mom left, we never went anywhere. Never had a car. Dad couldn't drive. We never had a holiday, never went to Greece or Majorca, never went anywhere at weekends, never did anything. . . .

"Hey!"

The bus had stopped and the bus driver was calling down the aisle.

"You getting off, or what?"

To get to the sea you have to walk down through this sleepy little village, along the coast road for a while, then turn left down some steep steps that lead to the beach. There was hardly anyone around, just a couple of old ladies creeping around on walking sticks and a decrepit old boatman with a half-dead dog. As

I moved on down the coast road, a lonely clinking sound drifted in from the rigging of small boats resting in the distant mud. Seagulls screeched and squabbled, circling aimlessly in the breeze.

The sky was dark and heavy.

As I stepped down onto the beach, the shingle crunched beneath my feet. It felt momentous, as if I'd stepped into another world. Away from civilization. Away from cars and houses and shops and buskers and Christmas carols and plywood reindeer . . . away from everything.

I felt happy, I don't know why. Perhaps it was the emptiness of the place. Cold, wild, unwelcoming. Raw and open. Hostile. Blameless.

The wind had died to almost nothing and the air was still. Icy cold bit into my bones. I buttoned my coat and pulled my woolly hat down over my ears and headed out along the beach. The sky seemed to lower itself to the ground as I followed the shoreline, walking slowly, head down, aiming for a distant point where the beach narrowed and disappeared into the sea. The farther I went, the quieter it became. The sea was heavy and calm and the shingle had merged into a fine dry sand that silently soaked up my steps.

I thought no harbored thoughts, just walked the shoreline kicking up jewels. Polystyrene, plastic, municipal junk. Driftwood. Floats. Take-out cartons. Sandals. Bones of fish heads. Razors, gapers, and whelks. Countless tiny seashells, flesh-pink and paper-thin. A thick stink filled the air as I passed the dull black carcass of a dead porpoise. Pale gray meat showed where the rubbery skin had been hacked open by the propeller of a boat. Ripped apart. I imagined it thrashing helplessly in the sea, screaming unintelligible screams.

Dying.

I paused, weighed down with a sudden sadness.

Snow began to fall. Big, fat, lazy flakes, fluttering, seesawing, circling, taking their time, riding down slowly through the cold thickness of the air. Soft white crystals as big as coins. A surge of excitement raced through me as I looked up into the sky and saw nothing but white darkness. Millions of snowflakes dropping from the sky like invaders from another planet, silent and serene — menacing.

It was awesome. An alien world.

As I gazed up into the sky I wondered how I'd look to God if He was up there. I imagined myself as a tiny black dot, a blind particle crawling through the snow and sand. An insect. Going nowhere. Alone. Indeterminate, immeasurable, and shapeless.

Nothing much at all.

I looked down and moved on. Forget it, I thought. Think of something else. Think of something solid. The sand, the snow . . . what is it? What's it made of? Come on, think. Sand. I don't know, rocks, stones, shells, fish bones, all smashed up by the sea, pulverized over millions of years. Sand. Sandcastle. Sandpiper. Invisible sandpiper. Sandpaper. Sandwich. Cheese sandwich. Cheese on toast. What about the snow? What's snow? What's it made of? Frozen rain? No, that's hailstones. Or is it? I don't know. Snow's made of crystals. Symmetrical patterns. Every snowflake is unique. Is it? How can you tell? Is there a record kept of every single snowflake that's ever fallen? There *might* be two that are the same. Who knows? Snow. Snowball. Snowdrop. Drop of snow. Snow goose. That's no goose, that's my wife. Snowshoe. Bless you. Snowman. Walking in the air. Abominable. Snow. Snow. Quick, quick, snow . . .

I looked up. Flat nothingness stretched out in front of me. White, gray, black, white, gray, black. Sand, sea, sky. I was hardly moving. It was like walking on a treadmill, walking but not getting anywhere. Time seemed to have disappeared. Not stopped or slowed down, just disappeared.

Forget it, I thought. Just keep walking. Keep moving. Keep thinking. Sea. The sea. Salt water. Brine. Brian. Call me Brian. Destiny. Sea. Adriatic Sea. South China Sea. Irish Sea. Red Sea. The Dead Sea. The dead see. Atlantic Sea? No, it's Atlantic *Ocean*. What's the difference between a sea and an ocean? I don't know, what is the difference between a sea and an ocean? I don't know. Sea. Seashell. Michelle. Seashore. Seasick. Sea slug. Seaweed. Sea dog. Salty sea dog, har har. Seaplane. Sea Scout. See you later, alligator. Sea anemone. See an enemy. What else? The sky. Hell, I don't know what the sky is. The sky's just the sky. The sky's the limit. Pie in the sky. Steak-and-kidney pie. Snake-and-pygmy pie. Sky diver. Skyscraper. Sky rocket. Skylark. Sky sandpiper. Sky piper. Sea piper. Invisible piper. . . .

I stopped. I was at the end of the beach. A finger of sand poked out into the muddy sea, and I was standing at the finger's end. There was nowhere else to go. The colorless sea stretched out endlessly in front of me, a blurred emptiness of water and snow, dark and cold and formless. I sat down on the rise of a shingle bank and stared, hypnotized, at the snow-filled sky.

If I sit here long enough, I thought, I'll die. I'll freeze to death. And tomorrow morning someone walking their dog will come along and find me sitting cross-legged at the edge of the sea, like a statue, frozen stiff. White without and white within. A snowman. Snowboy.

Would that be so bad? I wondered. Would it hurt?

I imagined the coldness eating into me, numbing my fingers, my nose, my toes, my ears, before gradually moving on to my limbs, my skin, my bones, until eventually my whole body would be frozen into a state of senselessness and I wouldn't feel anything at all.

Would that be so bad? I don't know.

Is it too late already?

Could I stand up even if I wanted to?

My legs are dead, they don't belong to me.

My thoughts are slowing.

What do you want to do?

What do you want to be?

What do you want?

I don't know.

I'm tired.

My eyes are heavy.

The snow falls.

Never ending.

Dark and light.

Black and white.

Good and bad.

Me and Dad.

Me and Alex.

There she is. I can see her. Gliding silently across the sea in a candle-white dress. I can see her. I can see her pale face and her shiny black hair, her dark eyes flecked with green. I can see her.

She's beautiful.

What do you want to do?

I want to reach out to her, to touch her, but I can't move. I want to call out to her, to call her name, but I have no voice. All I can do is watch her as she drifts across the sea and onto the sand, floating gently toward me, smiling her smile, coming closer, smiling at me, coming closer, and closer . . . and then she stops. Still smiling, she throws back her head and opens her mouth to swallow the falling snow, and white petals tumble from her hair. She looks at me again, and my heart cries. A tremor plays upon her lips and her eyelids flicker like excited wings as she holds out her hand and moves toward me. . . .

And then she changes.

It's not Alex. It never was. It's Dad. Staggering up the beach dressed ridiculously in size eight boots and a ragged white dress. Like a ghoulish scarecrow, deathly pale and drunk. Dad. With a can of shaving foam clutched in his outstretched hand spraying out fountains of creamy-white snow. Dad. The snow-maker. Lifeless but alive, dead eyes sunk into his wounded head, lurching up the sand with a boozy leer on his face, laughing his laugh, coming closer, laughing at me, coming closer and closer. . . .

My eyes sprang open and I jerked to my feet. With a violent shiver I slapped the snow from my limbs and stood there swaying on numbed and bloodless legs.

Look! Look out there! There's nothing there, just a cold black sea in the snow. There's nothing there, you idiot. Move. Now. Go on. Get out of here before you freeze to death.

What?

Move!

I turned and ran.

It was hard work. The wind was blowing again, gusting snow into my face, and I was hurting with cold. My legs were stiff and the wet sand dragged at my feet. It was like running through molasses — sandy white molasses. But I kept going, pumping my arms, breathing hard, sucking cold air into my lungs, and as the fresh oxygen rushed through my head the images of Dad and Alex began to crumble and fade. The eyes, the white dress, that smile . . .

Was that really Alex?

Was it a dream?

Was it real?

Forget it, the voice said. *Just run.*

Maybe it never happened at all? Maybe it was —

It was nothing. *You were cold, that's all. Cold, wet, and hungry. You haven't eaten much the last few days. You're tired. You dozed off. That's all. You're cold and tired. Your mind plays tricks. Forget it, just keep running.*

And I ran.

On and on, running blindly through the snow, head down, legs pounding, heart racing, running like I'd never run before. On and on through the sand and the snow and the wind and the sand and the snow and the wind and the sand . . . I lost all track of time. For all I knew, I could have been running forever. I'd forgotten why I was running in the first place. Was I running *away* from something or running *to* something? It didn't seem to matter. I was running, that's all. Just running. Through the sand and the snow and the wind and the sand and the snow and the wind . . . until eventually I felt solid ground beneath my feet.

The steps.

I hardly dared believe it. I stamped my feet, cautiously at first, then harder, grinning with mad delight at the reassuring clump of boots on concrete. Ha! Real, solid ground. Wonderful.

Hard, shiftless. Concrete. Tarmac. A *sensible* surface. A surface made for walking. I grabbed hold of the handrail and pulled myself up the steps and on to the road.

Here, everything was calm and quiet again. The sea was silent in the distance, the wind had dropped to a whisper, and the voice in my head had gone.

I looked up at the sky. The snow had stopped. It was just a sky.

I glanced back at the beach, but there was nothing to see. Just a gray-white haze. Nothing. Just a beach.

I headed slowly up the coast road.

The village was even more deserted than it had been when I'd arrived. No old women, no old boatman, no dog. It could have been a ghost village. Wet, dark, and deserted. I looked around for a shop. I needed food, a hot drink. A cup of tea and a Mars bar. But there was nothing. Everywhere was closed.

I wished I'd never come here.

The snow was already starting to melt on the road, oozing into the gutters like mashed potato swimming in gravy. I walked on through the mush up to the bus stop and sat down.

Wet feet. Wet bottom.

Wet bus-stop bench.

I settled down to wait for the bus.

I didn't know what time it was.

It was time to go home, that's what time it was.

I remember it now. Most of it. I think. I remember the snow. I remember the cold, but I don't *remember* the cold, because you can't remember stuff like that, can you? Cold, pain, fear — you can't remember feelings. You can remember the idea of something, you can remember that you were cold, you were in pain, you *were* afraid, but you can't actually *remember* the feeling of it.

It did happen, though.

I'm sure it did.

Believe it.

Or don't. It's up to you. I don't really care. I know what happened.

The light was low as I stepped off the bus and hurried home through the sludge. It felt like early evening. I wondered if Alex had stopped by yet. Had I missed her?

I should never have gone to the damned beach; it was a stupid idea in the first place. I should have stayed at home. Why did I go? What was I thinking of? Today was the day, *the* day. The day we planned to lose a body. And I go wandering off to the beach in the middle of a snowstorm. Good thinking, Martyn. Good idea. Very smart.

My clothes were still wet, shrunk so tight to my body I had to fight to get the door key out of my pants pocket. My fingers were all numb, too, white and wrinkled like I'd been lying in the bath too long.

Inside, the house was cold. I turned on all the lights, peeled off my coat, pulled off my wet boots and socks, and lit the fire.

Five past two, the clock said. Surely it was later than that? It must be wrong. I checked the clock in the kitchen. It was five past two. I couldn't believe it. I thought I'd been gone for ages.

Never mind.

Forget it, I told myself. Forget the whole thing. Just start again, pretend the day's just beginning.

I put the kettle on, made myself a big mug of tea, and got a packet of chocolate cookies from the cupboard. Then I went upstairs and ran a bath. A hot, hot bath. As I undressed I noticed myself in the mirror. Bleached-white with a hint of blue. Red ears, red nose, watery eyes. I looked like a newborn baby.

Blissfully, I sank down into the steaming hot water. The snow and the cold and the dirt and the bad memories just melted away. I gulped hot strong tea and munched chocolate cookies. I turned on the radio.

I was home.

Home is home, I suppose. No matter how much you hate it, you still need it. You need whatever you're used to. You need security.

I almost didn't hear the doorbell at first. With my head under the water and the radio on, it was just a muffled *brrrr*. I sat up, turned off the radio, and cocked my head to let the water out of my ears. This time it was clearer. *Brrring*. I jumped out, wrapped a towel around my waist, and sped downstairs. Wet footprints trailed behind me on the carpet.

"Alex!" I said, opening the door.

She looked me up and down, surprised. I tightened the towel, suddenly feeling embarrassed.

"I was in the bath," I said, letting her in.

She touched a finger to my face. "You've got chocolate on your chin."

I let go of the towel, wiped at my face, then grabbed the towel again as I felt it slip. Alex grinned. She was wearing an old fur hat with the earflaps hanging down, big fur boots, and a long black coat. All lightly frosted with sleet.

I shut the door.

"Look at you," Alex said, removing her hat.

I didn't know what she meant. I felt uncomfortable. Standing there, half-naked and wet. I must have looked like a freshly plucked chicken, scrawny and pale, bony legs hanging out from beneath the towel like knotted strings. Pigeon-chested, too. I was a birdman. Birdboy.

I slicked back my hair and it fell limply to one side. I didn't know what to do with my hands. I'd never stood half-naked in front of a girl before. Beneath the towel I felt . . . vulnerable. I think that's what I felt, anyway.

"I'll go and get dressed," I said.

Alex laughed. "I think you'd better."

I was just zipping up my pants when she waltzed into the bedroom pulling a couple of strappy-looking things from her bag.

"I brought these," she said.

What? I thought. Brought what? Don't you ever knock before you come in? I could have been naked.

"What are they?" I asked as she dangled whatever it was in my face.

"Surgical masks," she explained. "To keep the smell out."

She put one on. It was one of those masks that surgeons wear when they're operating.

"See?"

I was impressed. "Where did you get them from?"

"Mom's nursing stuff. I found them in her drawer. Here." She handed me one and I put it on, tying it at the back of my head. I looked in the mirror. Doctor Pig.

"It looks good on you," Alex said.

"Thanks."

"Covers up your face."

"Funny."

I went into the bathroom and got two pairs of rubber gloves from the cupboard under the sink, then went back into the bedroom and offered them to Alex.

"Pink or yellow?" I asked.

She looked confused.

"Fingerprints," I explained.

"Oh."

I smiled. "The downfall of many a criminal mind."

"Right."

"So, pink or yellow?"

She took the yellow ones and we gloved up.

"Where's the car?" I asked.

She looked at her watch. "Mom's not back yet. Another hour or so."

"That's all right. We've still got to get him downstairs, anyway."

She sighed. "Look, Martyn, are you sure about all of this? Isn't there some other way —"

"Don't worry about it," I said. "I've got it all worked out. Come on, I'll show you."

Dad's bedroom still smelled pretty rank, even with the masks on. There was a clamminess about the place — the bedding, the carpet, the air — and everything felt cold and untouchable.

I went to the bed, reached underneath, and tugged out a sleeping bag. Green, nylon, smelly. I unrolled it and laid it out on the floor.

"It zips up nearly all the way around," I said, showing her.

She knelt down beside me. "There's a gap at the top. His head'll poke out."

I pulled a stapler from my back pocket, grinning. "Click click."

Alex still wasn't happy. "What if they find him? The police. They could trace the sleeping bag back to you."

I shook my head. "It's never been used. Dad won it in a game of cards, years ago. He shoved it under the bed and forgot about it."

"A game of cards? How do you win a sleeping bag in a game of cards?"

"Don't ask me. Anyway, it's clean. Dirty, but clean, if you know what I mean. I know these things, Alex. I read murder mysteries."

"If you say so."

"I do."

We stood up and studied each other. Masked-up and rubber-gloved. Alex looked good in the mask, mysterious. Her eyes glinted darkly.

"OK then," I said. "Let's get him dressed. Where did you put his shirt and jacket?"

"I'll get them." She went briskly over to the wardrobe and opened it. "White shirt?"

I nodded. She passed me the shirt.

"And jacket."

I took the jacket from her, a grimy black thing. "Hold on."

"What?"

"I thought he was wearing his other one."

"What? What other one?"

"The brown one."

"Which brown one?"

I looked at her. "He's got two jackets. This one, and a mucky old brown one. I'm sure he was wearing the brown one. Have another look in the wardrobe, and see if it's there."

She hesitated. "What does it matter? I mean, it doesn't make any difference which jacket he's wearing, does it? Who's going to know?"

"Well, I suppose. It's just . . . I like to get the details right. It makes me feel —"

"That's the jacket he was wearing, Martyn. I remember it. OK? Now, let's get this finished." She shut the wardrobe and passed me Dad's shoes and socks. I was about to say something else about the jacket, but the look on her face said don't-you-dare, so I didn't.

After I'd got him dressed I unzipped the sleeping bag and laid it out next to the bed. Then I crossed to the other side of the bed and removed the duvet. Dad just lay there: mute, blind, unquestioning, pale, bloodless, dead. He seemed to have shrunk. Skin hung loosely from his frame, like the skin of a 100-year-old man. I imagined the skeleton beneath the covering of skin. Brittle white bones, calcium. Joined in all the right places, as if by magic.

Using a damp cloth I wiped all the makeup from his face. Underneath, his skin was the color of wet newspaper.

Then I stooped, gripped the edge of the mattress, and lifted. I didn't think he was going to move at first; I thought he was somehow stuck to the mattress. But then he began to roll. I raised the mattress higher and he fell to the floor with a dead thump.

Ouch, I thought.

I positioned him on top of the sleeping bag, then crouched down and took his hand in mine. His body wasn't stiff any more, but his hand felt hard and unforgiving, just as it had when he was alive. It was a hand I'd never really seen, not up close. I didn't know it. All it had ever been to me was something I got hit with. I stared at the lines and contours in the skin, the whorls on the fingertips, the hard, dirty fingernails, the stiff black hairs on the backs of his fingers. The skin was dirty, stained with dust. A small white scar at the base of the thumb stood out bright against the gray skin. On the middle finger of his right hand a dull gold ring was embedded into the flesh. I wondered where it was from. Was it a gift? Who gave it to him? Mom?

I dug into my pocket and brought out the envelope containing the hairs and the cigarette butt I'd collected from the kitchen floor. Carefully, I lodged some of Dean's hairs under one of Dad's fingernails, wrapping the long ends around the tip of his finger to help keep them in place. That should do it.

I crossed his arms over his chest.

I turned the envelope upside-down and scattered the rest of the hairs and the cigarette butt into the bag, then zipped it up. *Zip zip zip.* I tightened the drawstring and tied it off, then whipped out the stapler and stapled shut the top of the bag with a nice straight line of staples. *Chickchick chickchick chickchick.*

Gone.

I'd never see him again.

I stared down at the big green nylon cocoon and wondered if I ought to feel something. Anything.

But I didn't. There was nothing there.

"Might as well get him downstairs," I said. "You take that end."

The nylon material hissed on the carpet as we dragged the bag out of the bedroom, into the hallway, and then across to the top of the stairs where we stopped to catch our breath.

"Heavy," panted Alex.

I nodded, sucking in air.

The bottom of the stairs looked a long way away, a long way down.

"There's not much point in carrying him down," I said.

She shrugged. "Suppose not."

I moved down a couple of stairs, turned and grabbed the end of the sleeping bag, took a deep breath, and tugged. The bag slid slowly over the edge of the top stair and stopped. Jammed.

"Give it a push," I said.

Alex bent down and pushed from behind while I reached over and grabbed a handful of nylon and pulled. The bag bent in the middle as I pulled it up into a sitting position.

"And again," I said.

She pushed, I pulled. The bag moved forward, tottered for a second, then suddenly lurched toward me.

"Watch out!"

I jumped to one side just in time to watch it tumble past me and clatter down the stairs — *clump clomp clomp clomp clumpclump clump clompclump kathump*. It landed at the bottom of the stairs in a heap.

From the front room window I watched a fine sleet slanting down into the street. Alex's mom had returned ten minutes ago,

I'd seen her driving by. Alex had called her to check what time she was going out. Six o'clock. We had another hour.

Alex lay stretched out on the couch sucking an orange. "How are we going to get him in the car?" she asked.

It was a good question. The sort of question a good murder mystery writer ought to have an answer to. I didn't have a clue.

"Martyn?"

"What?"

"How are we going to get him in the car?"

"I don't know," I admitted.

How would it be done in a story? I racked my brains, trying to remember if I"d ever read anything similar. The only thing I could think of was a story about a man who'd murdered his wife and hid the body in the woods, but that was out in the wilds somewhere, in a log cabin or something, up in the mountains, somewhere deserted. This was slightly different. A terraced house in a cramped side street in a nosy neighborhood.

"At least it's dark," Alex said.

I gazed through the window. Sleet shone in the glare of the street lamp across the road. It's never dark around here, I thought. There's lights everywhere you look. Streetlights, bright white security lights, car headlights, so much light you can hardly see the stars at night.

"We'll just have to take a chance," I said. "Bring the car up as close to the door as possible, then get him into the car quickly and hope that no one sees."

"Hope that no one sees?" Alex repeated incredulously.

"Unless you've got a better idea?"

She leaned back and stared at the ceiling. Her hair was tied back, and beneath it her neck was pale and slender, like a sleek white tube. As she reached around to adjust her ponytail I suddenly thought of Dean. An image of his pudgy face floated into my mind. Slack features, loose mouth, lizard eyes, stupid hair. Dean . . . I hadn't forgotten about him, I'd just put him to one side for the moment. One thing at a time. That's the way to do it. One thing at a time. Once this business was over I'd get back to Dean. Oh, yes.

I wondered what Alex thought of him now. How did she feel about what he'd done? Angry? Humiliated? Embarrassed? It was impossible to tell with Alex. She liked to keep her emotions to herself.

"Well?" I said.

She sat up and wiped her fingers on a tissue. "I can't think of anything."

I smiled. "We'll just have to take a chance, then, won't we?"

It doesn't really matter, I thought, as I dragged the bagged Dad to the front door and waited for Alex to bring the car around. If someone sees us, they see us. If they don't, they don't. That's all there is to it. It's that mysterious tune again, the invisible piper. He plays, we dance — what happens, happens.

I still had the rubber gloves on, but not the mask. I thought that might be just a bit *too* suspicious. Over the rubber gloves I wore another pair of woolly fingerless ones. I also wore my old parka, with its fur-lined hood, a thick sweater, woolly hat, boots, and long thick socks. I'd had more than enough of being cold and wet today, thank you very much.

I heard Alex starting up the car down the road. It whined,

chugged for a bit, then coughed and died. She tried it again —
urrurrurr . . . urrurrurr . . . urrurrurreeow . . . then silence. Why
couldn't her mom have a decent car? Something Japanese.
Something that worked properly. I cringed as the whining
started up again, but this time, after a couple of seconds, the
engine roared into life. Well, not roared, exactly, but it started.
Alex revved up the engine, pumping it like a maniac, keeping it
going, then I heard a crunching sound as she looked for the
right gear, followed by the squeak of the emergency brake, then
more revving, more crunching. . . . Why did she have to make so
much noise?

A couple of minutes later I heard the car pull up outside the
front door. Emergency brake on, engine idling. I opened the
door and there it was — Dad's hearse: a dirty old van covered in
rust and coughing out smoke.

It seemed strangely appropriate.

Alex was standing by the open back doors. In her snow-
covered fur hat and big fur boots she looked like an eskimo.
Eskimo Alex.

"Do you think there's enough room?" she shouted out over
the noise of the engine.

"Shhh!" I said, holding a finger to my lips.

"What?" she shouted.

I beckoned her to the door.

"Keep your voice down."

"Sorry," she said, lowering her voice. "Do you think there's
enough room?"

I looked in the back of the car. "Easy."

Headlights swept around the corner and a car full of loud

music and tough guys drove past, swooshing too fast through the fresh snow. I went to close the door but it was too late, they were gone. It didn't matter, anyway, there was nothing to see. A couple of young kids and a beat-up old car . . . so what?

"Come on," I said. "Let's get him in and get going." One last glance up and down the street. "OK?"

"OK."

I reached down and grabbed the head end of the sleeping bag, Alex got the other end and we shuffled out the door as quick as we could. Now that the body had loosened up a bit it wasn't quite so awkward to maneuver, but it was sagging a lot more, and that seemed to make it even heavier. The weight strained at my back and I kept reminding myself to take small steps. It's best to take small steps when you're carrying something heavy.

The car was parked half on and half off the curb, tilted at a slight angle.

"Put him down a second," I whispered as we got to the back of the car.

I adjusted my hold, got underneath the bag so I could lift it up easier.

"I'll get this end in first, then we'll swing the rest up after."

Alex nodded, although I'm not sure she heard me. The engine was chugging away, exhaust fumes billowing out into our faces, snow tumbling down, both of us struggling with the weight, gasping for breath. I heard a door slam somewhere but didn't dare to look. Just get him in, I thought, just get him in and go. I heaved with all my strength and threw my end of the sleeping bag into the back of the car. *Thump.* Alex lost her grip on the other end and the whole thing started to slide out but I grabbed it just in time and then together we just about managed to shove it back in.

I slammed the doors shut.

"All right?" I asked breathlessly.

She nodded, tight-lipped.

"Let's go."

On the way around to the passenger's door I had that stupid feeling that if I kept my head down I couldn't be seen. I fought against it and raised my eyes from the ground to risk a quick look up the street, then down. Nothing. Empty. Snow. Streetlights. Curtains closed. No one looking. I got in the car and pulled the door shut.

Alex was reaching beneath her seat, tugging a lever, trying to pull the seat further forward. It wouldn't move.

"Darn it!"

She pulled harder and the seat shot forward jamming her legs up against the steering wheel.

"Darn!"

She pushed it back, got it where she wanted it, then grabbed hold of the gearstick with both hands and started shoving it around, cursing intently, her cold breath misting in the air.

"Get in, get in, stupid thing —"

"Take it easy," I said, "there's no hurry now."

"Stupid thing . . . there!" She whacked the car into gear and grabbed hold of the steering wheel.

"Alex!" I said.

"I can't see anything!"

Snow covered the windshield.

"Alex!" I grabbed her arm.

"What?" Her face was red and her eyes panicky.

"Calm down. There's no need to rush. Put the wipers on."

She flicked a switch and the headlights went out.

"Darn."

She flicked them on again, mumbling to herself. "Wipers, wipers, wipers . . ."

I reached across and pulled a lever and the wipers scraped slowly across the windshield, clearing a hole in the snow.

Alex turned to me, her face cold and frightened.

"It's all right," I said. "Just take it easy."

The iciness melted and she smiled. "Sorry."

"We don't want to get stopped," I said. "It might be a bit hard to explain what we're doing."

She wiped a hand across her face. "Yeah, I'm sorry. I'll be all right now."

The snow was really coming down now, which was both good news and bad news. Good, because it meant there wouldn't be many people around; and bad, because I didn't look forward to driving through a snowstorm in a wreck of a car, with a dead body in the back, driven by an underage wreck of a driver, with no license and no insurance.

"Nice and easy," I said. "Not too fast and not too slow. OK?"

"No problem."

We pulled away with a jerk, accelerated down the street then slid around the corner at the bottom, missing a parked car by inches.

We were on our way.

We kept to the back roads as much as possible. Alex was grim and silent, concentrating on her driving, her head pressed right up close to the windshield, squinting out into the blurred white blackness. Every now and then she'd press her head even closer to the windshield and say, "Where's the road? Where's the blasted road gone?" I couldn't tell, it all looked the same to me: road, snow, sky, hedges, trees. It was all just *outside*. I didn't have a clue. Alex seemed to manage, though, jerking the steering wheel this way and that, braking, juggling gears, cursing quietly to herself.

I just sat there and stared through the windshield, letting my mind wander.

Four days to go until Christmas. I tried to imagine what I'd be doing on Christmas Day. In the house, watching television on my own? Watching all those terrible Christmas Specials and the same old stupid films, eating too much, making myself sick? No, I thought. Not this time. By Christmas Day I'd be somewhere else. Somewhere else. Another town, another country, even. Somewhere hot, a beach, palm trees, blue skies. With Alex. She'd be strolling around in a bikini, sipping from a cool drink, and I'd be lounging around doing nothing, getting a tan, dressed in an old straw hat and a pair of long baggy shorts. Then later on I might mosey out along the beach on my own, go for a swim, maybe a bit of surfing —

"Martyn?"

We'd stopped at a T in the road.

"Which way?"

I looked out of the window, trying to work out where we were, but all I could see was snow and tall roadside hedges. Left or right? Left looked as if it might take us back toward town. I didn't know why, it just did. The road to the right looked as if it *might* be the road down to the pub where Dad had left his wallet that time. The old quarry should be around here somewhere. I rolled down the window to get a better look. Snow gusted into my face.

"Martyn!"

I rolled up the window.

"Which way?" she asked. "I thought you knew the way?"

"I do," I said. "If I knew where we were, I'd know which way to go."

"Great."

The inside of the car suddenly lit up and we both turned to see headlights approaching from behind.

"Crap," said Alex.

"Go right."

"Are you sure?"

The car pulled up behind us.

"Just go."

She slammed the car into gear and pulled out to the right. I watched in the rearview mirror as the car behind us signaled left and pulled away.

"It's gone," I said.

We drove on. The further we went, the less sure I was that we were going in the right direction.

"Where the hell are we?" Alex moaned. "If we carry on like this we'll be driving around all night."

"I think we should have gone left," I said.

"What?"

"I think I know where we are now. We should have turned left at the T. You'll have to stop and turn around."

She said nothing, but I could tell she was fuming. The road

was getting narrower and narrower, thick hedges closing in. There was nowhere to turn.

"Sorry," I said.

Suddenly she stepped on the brakes and swung on the steering wheel. The car veered toward the hedge.

"Wha —"

"There's a gate."

I don't know how she spotted it but she was right. There was a gateway into a field, just big enough to stop and turn around in. She found reverse, shot out backward into the road, wheels spinning in the snow, and then we were off again, back the way we'd come.

I glanced across and saw her smiling. "Not bad," I said.

She nodded. "Just don't get us lost again."

At the T I told her to drive straight on. The road dipped then rose again up a long steep hill. Halfway up the engine began to shudder.

"Change gear," I suggested.

"I already have."

We were doing about 10 mph.

"Turn left at the top," I said.

I could see the tips of cranes in the distance, dim stalks poking up into the night. The quarry. We drove down the hill, past the pub, then up again, the engine moaning at the strain. Along another narrow lane, more tall black hedges, signs warning of concealed entrances. I peered out through the windshield, looking for the track to the gravel pit. It was here somewhere.

"Slow down," I said.

We slowed.

"There."

"Where?"

"There, on the left."

She almost missed it, pulling in at the last moment to stop beside a rusted iron gate.

"Is this it?"

"Turn off the lights. I'll open the gate."

I stepped out into the cold blackness. The ground beneath my feet was frozen solid. Driving wind blasted snow into my face. I checked that no cars were coming, pulled up my hood and crossed to the gate, opened it, then signaled Alex to reverse through. As she maneuvered the car I kept an eye out for traffic. There was nothing. No cars, no lights, just the long black ribbon of the road slicing dimly through the barren landscape. Wasteland, that's all it was. Acres of used-up land, scraped, dug out, exhausted. Just a big hole on the outskirts of town.

I hurried back to the car and got in.

"OK," I said.

"Where?"

I pointed through the rear windows. "Down there."

"It's a bit dark, isn't it?"

I shrugged.

"There's nothing there, Martyn, it's pitch black."

"Just drive," I said. "It's straight down."

"Are you sure?"

"Trust me."

We reversed slowly, very slowly, down the track, both of us twisted around in our seats peering out through the rear windows into the gloom. Alex was right, it was *extremely* dark. No moon, no stars, just darkness everywhere. We inched backward down the track, the engine making that peculiar high-pitched whine of reversing. There was something oddly comforting about it.

"How much farther?"

"Not far," I said, hoping I was right.

"If we back into a huge hole full of icy water —"

"Just watch where you're going, Alex."

"I am!"

I thought I caught a glimpse of something. Something blacker than everything else.

"Stop!"

She stabbed the brakes. The car skidded alarmingly for a few long seconds then stopped.

"Is that it?" she asked.

I squinted into the dark. Was there anything there? I shut my eyes, then opened them again. Maybe.

"Can you see anything?" I asked.

"I think so . . . just down there?"

As my eyes adjusted to the dark, the shadows became clearer. A hole in the ground. Deep. Black. Steep-sided. Big enough to swallow a bus and a bit too close for comfort.

We looked at each other.

"That's it," I said.

"Rocks."

"What?"

I peered into the darkness. "Where are you?"

"Here."

I couldn't see her. "We need some rocks."

"What for?"

I looked toward the sound of her voice and saw a dim outline standing at the edge of the gravel pit, looking down.

"Weights," I said, crossing over to where she stood. "To weigh down the sleeping bag, otherwise it'll float."

"I don't think so," she said.

I followed her gaze and looked down into the hole. Solid ice glinted in the pitch-black depths. Alex picked up a pebble and lobbed it over the edge. We waited . . . and heard a hollow clatter as the pebble hit the ice, bounced, then skittered across the frozen surface.

"Rocks," I said again.

We scrambled around in the freezing dark looking for rocks. It was still snowing like mad, cold as anything. The ground was uneven, slippery, icy-hard. Dead roots and bits of old machinery jutted out all over the place. And it was dark as hell.

But I felt great. My mind was crystal clear, I knew exactly what I was doing. The cold, the dark, the danger — it didn't matter. I was focused. I was doing what had to be done. That's all. I was *doing* it. For the first time in my life I was really *doing* something.

After about ten minutes we had a fair-sized pile of rocks. I stooped down and picked out a really big one, lifted it with both hands, and heaved it over the side of the gravel pit. This time we heard a satisfying crack — a flat, brittle snap that echoed dully off the walls of the pit — followed instantly by the massive splash of the rock smashing through the ice.

"I love that sound," I said.

Another half dozen or so rocks went over the side until I was pretty sure the ice was all smashed up.

"That'll do," I said. "Let's get him out."

Alex opened the car's rear doors and I reached in, grabbed hold of the sleeping bag, and dragged it out. It fell to the ground with a cold thump. I squatted down and unzipped it just a little at the side.

"Rocks," I said.

Alex passed me the rocks and I stuffed them into the bag. A car droned past on the road above us and we both froze for an instant. Twin yellow headlights appeared, lighting up the falling snow, then they were gone. I kept filling the bag with rocks.

"What's the time?" I asked.

She held her wristwatch up to her eyes. "Quarter to eight."

I put one more rock in the bag, then zipped it up. "Give me a hand," I said. "We'll have to drag it."

We both stooped and took hold of a corner of the sleeping bag.

"Ready?"

She nodded.

"One, two, three — pull!"

It was a lot heavier now, loaded with rocks, but once we got going it wasn't too bad, and after four or five big tugs we reached the edge of the pit.

We must have looked like something out of an old horror film: a graveyard scene, midwinter, the dead of night, two hunchbacks dragging a body in a rock-filled sack across the icy ground . . .

I smiled at the image.

A sliver of moon had appeared from behind the dark shroud of snow clouds. Silent and pale. For a few moments the quarry landscape was dimly visible. Great mounds of dead earth, hacked-out trenches, flat and barren plains, empty oil drums, machinery remains, rusted cranes, crumbling cliffs. Here and there, nature was reclaiming the land. Clumps of wild grass swayed in the wind and the ground was dotted with dark and squat-looking shrubs. The wasteland was being reborn. It was all twilight gray, colorless in the pale light of snow and moon. Then the clouds closed and the moonlight was lost and everything was black again.

"Are you all right, Martyn?" Alex asked quietly.

I looked down into the depths of the gravel pit: The water waited, cold and deep and dark.

"Never felt better," I said.

Then I raised my foot and heaved the sleeping bag over the edge.

Silence.

The wind whistled faintly through the grasses.

A huge *kersplash* sounded from below.

I listened. Gurgling noises, bubbling, the sound of sinking. In my mind I saw the sodden sleeping bag drifting slowly down through the deep black icy water. Dad, zipped up and dead, senseless, tumbling in slow motion, sinking down through the cold dark liquid, finally coming to rest among the rocks and silt and supermarket trolleys and rusted bike frames at the bottom of the pit. Motionless and silent, cocooned, unseen in the frozen ooze.

Buried.

Gone.

Not sleeping, just dead.

. . .

Back in the car, Alex turned the ignition key. The engine whined, coughed, and died. She tried again. Nothing.

"It's all right," she said. "It always does this."

She pulled out the choke and tried again. This time the engine caught and she kept it revving, blue-gray exhaust smoke clouding out into the wind. She jammed it into gear, released the emergency brake and pressed the accelerator. The back wheels started spinning. I felt the car skid around to one side and slide back toward the gravel pit. We were going to join Dad in his watery grave . . . but Alex kept up the revs and suddenly we lurched forward and were away. No trouble.

Up the hill, through the gate. We stopped. I jumped out and closed the gate behind us, took one final look into the darkness below, then got back into the car.

"Let's go," I said.

We pulled out onto the road and I sank down in the seat and watched the wipers click-clack hypnotically across the windshield. Snowflakes fell and were wiped away, fell and were wiped away, fell and were wiped away — *click-clack, click-clack, click-clack*. Metronomic. The car was warm, heated by the working of the engine. Warm and close. Dozy. The engine droned sleepily and the tires whooshed faintly on the snow-covered road. Outside, the blur of hedges and falling snow passed by, back to where we'd come from. I felt a warm glow of comfort. Satisfied, happy, secure.

We were going home.

We'd done it.

I'd done it.

. . .

It probably sounds a lot worse than it actually was. What I did. But you'd be surprised what you can do when you have to. You'd be surprised how easy things are. Once you've accepted something's got to be done, no matter what it is, you can usually do it. You just *do* it. That's the way it is. And, anyway, what did I do that was wrong? You tell me. What did I do? Who did I hurt? I hurt nobody. It's not as if I broke any commandments or anything. Where does it say, "Thou shalt not bury thy father in a gravel pit"? Break it down, look at it, analyze my actions. What did I do? Did I kill? Did I steal? Did I commit adultery? Did I covet my neighbor's ass? Did I honor my father? Maybe not. But why the hell should I? He never honored me. What it all boils down to is: I never hurt anyone. And that's what it's all about, isn't it? Hurt and pain. Physical, mental, whatever else kind of hurt there is. *That's* what's bad. You can do just about anything you want — as long as it doesn't hurt anyone, or anything, it's probably OK.

A long straight road stretched out ahead. Parallel lines of hazy white lights drawing us into the outskirts of town. Nearly there.

"Alex?"

"Mmm?"

"How do you feel?"

She glanced across at me. "About what?"

"About Dean."

Her lips tightened and she turned her attention back to the road. "I don't want to talk about it."

"I only want to know how you feel about him."

"*What?*"

"How do you feel?"

"How do you *think* I feel?"

"I don't know, that's why I'm asking."

She changed gear angrily. "I feel terrible, that's how I feel. He's a bastard. All right? I hate him."

"You must have liked him before, though."

"Yeah?"

"Otherwise you wouldn't have gone out with him."

"You wouldn't understand."

"I might."

I watched her from the corner of my eye. Her face was a mask.

"You're too young," she snapped. "You wouldn't understand."

I don't think she meant it nastily, it just came out that way.

"How can I understand if you don't tell me?" I asked quietly.

She frowned at the windshield.

"Look," she said, "it's just . . . I know what he's like, OK? I always did. He's stupid . . . boring . . . selfish. I know that. He's not even good-looking. I *know*."

"So why did you go out with him?"

"Because . . ."

"Because what?"

"Just *because*, Martyn! All right? Just because."

I thought it was best to leave it there. She was either going to lose her temper or start crying if I carried on. Anyway, I had a pretty good idea what she was talking about and I didn't really want to hear it. But before I shut up, I had one more thing to say.

"He's not going to get the money, though, is he?"

Slowly, she turned to me and smiled. A grim, determined

smile. "Oh, no," she said. "He won't be getting the money." And then she laughed, a curiously cold sound, almost vicious. If it had been anyone else but Alex, I think it might have scared me.

We rode the rest of the way home in silence, each of us lost in our own little world. I was tired — exhausted. Too tired to think. It had been a long day. A very long day. My legs ached. All that walking on the beach, all that running. Was that only this morning? It seemed like a lifetime ago. Briefly, the memory of Dad in his scarecrow dress flashed into my mind. The snowmaker, staggering up the beach. Christ. I dismissed the image. Whatever had happened had happened. It was over. Done. Gone. Forget it. Think of something else.

There was too much to think about. I just wanted to get home and go to bed. Tomorrow I'd think about things. Sunday's a good day for thinking. It's quiet. I'd spend a quiet day thinking, working things out. On my own. In my house, on my own. Nobody but me. No body. Just me.

"You'd better drop me here," I said as we drove down the hill toward our street. "Best not to be seen together in the car."

"It's a bit late for that," said Alex.

She stopped, anyway. I stepped out. The night sky had cleared. The snow had stopped falling. Stars shone in their thousands. Cosmic dust.

My legs felt a bit unsteady as I leaned in through the door. "I'll see you tomorrow."

"OK," she said.

I slammed the door, stood to one side, and watched as the car careened away down the road, signaled right, then left, then swung out into the middle of the road and turned right into our street.

I put my hands in my pockets and looked up at the stars. Everything is determined, the beginning as well as the end, by forces over which we have no control.

Well, I thought to myself, that's that.

SUNDAY

Clingclangclong, clingclangclong, clingclangclongclong . . . Stupid church bells. Every Sunday morning they're at it, darn bell ringers, clanging away like lunatics. I wouldn't mind if they knew what they were doing, but they don't, they don't even know any tunes. All they do is *clingclangclong, clingclangclong,* hour after hour, the same old racket over and over again — *clingclangclong, cling, cling, clingclangclongclong.* Don't they know it's Sunday? People are trying to sleep.

The bell tower's in the church on the other side of the main road, opposite the timber yard. A dirty old place: The roof's covered with sheets of blue plastic and you can hardly see the walls for rusted scaffolding. There's a graveyard out front, overgrown and abandoned, where crumbling gravestones lean drunkenly in a jungle of rampant weeds. It's a ghost church. No one ever goes there, apart from the bell ringers. I saw them once, a bunch of sad-looking vegetarian types with beards and long arms. Bell ringer's arms. Perhaps that's where they drink — the Bell ringer's Arms. Ho ho.

It was nearly eleven o'clock.

Despite the cold, I'd left all the windows open during the night. Under the duvet I was warm and snug, while my exposed face tingled pleasantly in the icy breeze. I lay there and breathed in the cold air, sucking it right down into my lungs. It didn't smell of anything — no cigarette smoke, no stale beer, no whisky, no sweaty clothes, no VapoRub, no dead bodies — just cold December air.

Beautiful.

The bells stopped ringing and a dead silence descended. A snowy silence. You can tell when it's been snowing, it soaks up all the sounds, deadens everything. This was a snowy silence. I lay there and listened to it. A soft white sound.

After a while I dragged myself out of bed.

It was freezing. I skipped naked to the window and checked outside. I was right. The street lay covered in snow. Crisp and white, unbroken. I smiled. Everything was clean and white — cars, walls, the road, the pavement. All the muck and the dirt was hidden beneath a pure white blanket of snow.

It wouldn't last long, though. Cars driving up and down, people out with their shovels and brooms, salt trucks spreading sand and salt all over the place — by this afternoon it'd just be a wet, gray, mushy mess. Why can't they just leave it alone? It's only snow. It's not a plague of locusts or anything. It's the same with fallen leaves in the autumn. Why can't people just leave them be? Why does everybody rush around dementedly sweeping up every little leaf that falls to the ground? Sweep 'em up, brush 'em up, pile 'em up, and burn 'em. Burn the buggers! Burn them all before it's too late!

They're all crazy.

I closed the window and got dressed.

I made boiled eggs and toast for breakfast. Three eggs and four slices of toast. And a pot of tea. A *pot*, not just a cup, with real tea, loose, out of a packet. I couldn't remember how many spoonfuls you're supposed to use. Someone once told me: one for each cup and one for the pot. Is that right? I put two spoonfuls in the pot but it didn't seem like enough so I put another one in. I could do whatever I liked. I even set the table in the kitchen. Tablecloth, place mat, teaspoon, salt and pepper.

What else? The radio. I turned on the radio and turned the sound down low. Desert Island Discs murmured in the background. While I waited for the eggs to boil, I asked myself what I'd take if *I* was stranded on a desert island. I wouldn't bother with any records, for a start. If you've only got eight, you're going to get fed up with all of them pretty soon. They'd start to get on your nerves. So, no records. That left me with a book and a luxury object. What book would I take? Sherlock Holmes? Raymond Chandler? Agatha Christie? There's tons of books I really like, but what'd be the point? One book's not much good. Once you've read it half a dozen times you might as well throw it away. No, I wouldn't take a book, either. That left me with a luxury object. Luxury object? Something of no practical value. What? What do I like? What do I really like? Think. Come on, Martyn, there must be *something*? I stared into the pan of boiling water and watched the eggs bobbling about in the heat. Steam drifted up into my eyes. Water bubbling, eggs bobbling, tapping against the side of the pan. Luxury object? I couldn't think of anything. Nothing. There was nothing I wanted on my desert island, nothing at all.

The egg timer dinged and I turned off the gas.

After breakfast I went into the living room. Now that I was alone, it was quiet. Wonderfully quiet. But strangely unfamiliar. Like it was someone else's room. There was something about it, I don't know what. It was the same old front room — dim, slightly battered, out of date — but there was something different about it. Something . . . the light, maybe, cutting in through the window, snow-bright and clear. Bright, but not bright enough to spoil the darkness. No, it wasn't the light. Perhaps it was the room itself? I sprawled out on the sofa and let my gaze wander around the room, studying things, taking it all in. I looked at the bare walls. The thinning wallpaper, dull-green and lifeless, faded by years of weak sunlight, almost see-through. I looked at Dad's armchair, my armchair. High-backed, worn, a sort of grubby-brown/grayish color, the color you get when you mix all the colors in the paintbox together. The armchair just sat there looking back at me like a beat-up dog whose master has died. Forlorn. I looked away. Opposite the chair the big old television perched stupidly on its four tapered legs — like something out of the 1950s, a joke television. A square-eyed monster with big fat control knobs down one side. We didn't have a remote control. I'd once asked Dad if we could get one. He told me not to be so bloody weak, remote controls are for girls.

I turned my head to the floor and looked down at the carpet and saw a mirror-image of the walls — pale green, worn-thin, and sorry. Above me, the ceiling — yellowy-white, clouded with nicotine like a poisonous sky.

It's amazing how you can live somewhere for years without ever really *knowing* it.

Against the far wall a wooden cabinet stood tall and rigid, like a dark sentinel. Dad was so proud of it. "That's oak, you know," he used to say. But it wasn't. The glass doors were always locked, as if there was something of value inside. There wasn't. Just knickknacks, cheap porcelain figures, empty plate stands, a pewter beer mug engraved with someone else's name, a darts trophy, a presentation coin set with half the coins missing. A lazy collection of junk.

The telephone table by the door, scuffed and dull. Ragged bits of paper scrawled with telephone numbers, two chewed ballpoint pens in a plastic pot. And the telephone, mute and black, still waiting. *Go on, before it's too late.*

It was too late.

Then the fireplace. Artificial fire, artificial coal, dulled brass fireguard. False flames, unreal orange, unwarm. A cold fire. When it wasn't turned on it was the coldest-looking thing in the world. To one side, a chipped vase with a bent poker in it. Brick-red floor tiles. That gray-stone surround. Uniform cubes stuck together in an ugly jigsaw. The fireplace. I remembered the sound, bone on stone, that hollow crack. Bloodstone. Cold and hard and clean and deadly.

And on the mantelpiece above the fire the clock ticked slowly.

Twelve o'clock.

This room.

Something. I don't know what it was. It wasn't real.

• • •

I reached for the phone and dialed Alex's number. A deep, throaty voice answered. "Hello?"

"Mrs. Freeman?"

"Hello, Martyn. How are you?"

"Fine, thanks. Is Alex there?"

"She went out about an hour ago."

"Oh."

The line was silent.

"Do you know where she went?"

"No, sorry."

"Oh."

"Shall I tell her you called?"

"OK."

"I'll tell her when she gets in."

"OK."

"'Bye, then."

I put the phone down.

I had some thinking to do, anyway. I had to work on my plan. Like most plans, it wasn't perfect, but it was close enough. The trick with plans is that you have to take into account unforeseen circumstances. However well you work things out, there's always a chance that something you hadn't thought of will happen. Something unexpected. So what you have to do is work out all the possibilities — what if *this* happened, what if *that* happened, what if *this* happened and then *this* happened and then *that* happened? Of course, it's impossible to think of everything — there's a billion things that *could* happen — but what you have to make sure of is that you're prepared for things to suddenly shoot off in another direction. Contingency plans, that's the thing. It's no good just relying on Plan A, no matter how good you think it is. You've got to have more up your sleeve than that. You need a Plan B, a Plan C, a Plan D, E, F, G . . . You need a whole alphabet of plans. You've got to be ready.

Two hours later, all thought out, I called Alex again. The dial tone rang unanswered. The sound of an empty house.

Well.

I hate that. Not knowing where someone is. It bothers me.

Five o'clock. It was dark now. Sunday-afternoon-in-December dark. Winter dark. It comes down quick — I watched it from the bedroom window. Sunset. The bloodred disk of the sun outlined against a flat sky, the sky a dull glow of pearl-gray light. The sinking sun throwing out threads of color as it dies, reaching up into the dark, like a drowning man throwing up his arms, reaching out for something that isn't there. Then down it goes, vast and perfect, burning down into the sunrise of another time, another world. And when it's gone, the patient black water of the night steals in and up crawls the moon.

I watched it. I watched it all. I watched the colors. I watched the stars. I watched the movement of the skies. It made me realize just how small I am.

I called Alex again at six. This time I really let it ring. Still no answer. I let it ring some more, imagining the lonely echo of the phone at the other end. *Pheep-pheep, pheep-pheep, pheep-pheep* . . . Was anybody listening?

I placed the telephone, still ringing, on the table, went out into the hall, put on my hat and coat and went outside. Dusty snow feathered in the air, blown from the roofs of houses. Head down, I crossed the street, kicking idly at browned lumps of snow, and headed down toward Alex's house. I stopped outside. No car, no lights. Curtains drawn. I listened, heard the faint pheeping of the telephone. That's me, I smiled. I stood there for a while, just looking, checking it out. There was no one home. I turned around and walked back home.

I turned on the television, clicked through the channels, then turned it off again. The sound of it was irritating: everybody shouting, stupid music, commercials. *I feel like chicken tonight.* . . .

I turned out the lights and sat there.

Unexplained sounds flickered in the background — a wooden creak from upstairs, a faint hum, something shifting somewhere — shadow noises. I took no notice. That kind of thing doesn't bother me. Ghosts and stuff, spooky business, there's nothing to it. It doesn't happen. Only in films and books. Not in real life.

Dad was dead, that was all. Gone. The thing lying in a sleeping bag at the bottom of a deep pool, that was just a wet sack of bones and meat. That was nothing to do with anything. An empty wrapper. Whatever it was that Dad was — his self, his being, his soul, call it what you like — had drifted away like a wisp of smoke the second his head hit the fireplace. Just drifted away. Where? Who knows? Who cares? Not me. Wherever it went, it wasn't here.

This house is empty.

Nine o'clock.

I watched the second hand tick slowly around the clock dial.

Then I watched the minute hand, staring hard, trying unsuccessfully to catch its movement.

Five past nine.

At nine-thirty a car pulled up across the street. I jogged upstairs to my bedroom and peeked through a gap in the curtains, hoping to see Alex and her mom. But it wasn't them. It was a dark-colored Escort. Two men sat in the front, faces dimly lit by the interior light. Both in their early twenties, one with a bush of frizzy red hair and a pockmarked face, the other dark and angular. I didn't recognize them. They were talking. Red opened some kind of wallet or bag and passed something to the dark one. Money? Red laughed, revealing a mouth full of strong white teeth. The other one cupped his hand to a lighter and lit a cigarette. Then they both got out of the car, slammed the doors, and slouched off down the snow-packed road, nodding their heads and muttering to each other. Off to Don's, I thought. Don's a drug dealer. He lives in a shabby old terraced house just off the main road. The curtains are always drawn and a huge white dog barks like mad whenever you pass the front door. Don's all right, though. I see him sometimes walking his dog down by the river. He always smiles and nods at me, bug eyes rolling all over the place. He's all right. His customers often park in the street outside our house. Less conspicuous than on the main road, I suppose.

I watched the car for a while to see if they came back, but they didn't. The street remained still and quiet.

I let the curtain drop and lay down on the bed.

When I was a little kid I used to think about dying. I'd lie in bed at night with my head beneath the covers trying to imagine the total absence of everything. No life, no darkness or light, nothing to see, nothing to feel, nothing to know, no time, no where or when, no nothing, forever. It was so unimaginable it was terrifying. I'd lie there for hours staring long and hard into the dark, looking for the emptiness, but all I'd ever see was black black black stretching deep into space for a million miles, and I knew it wasn't enough. I knew that when I died there'd be no black and no million miles, there wouldn't even be nothing, there'd be less than nothing, and the thought of that would fill my eyes with tears.

The tears have dried up over the years, but every now and then they come back, and when they do I realize that nothing much has changed — I'm still that little kid lying in bed at night looking for the emptiness.

Fourteen years I've slept in this room. Slept, read, daydreamed, cried. It used to be crowded full of stuff — toys, games, boxes full of comics, clothes, pictures, posters — but I threw most of it out about a year ago. All my old stuff. I just got fed up with it. One Saturday afternoon I got a couple of those big green garden garbage bags, the extra-strong ones, and piled everything I didn't want anymore into them. Then I lugged the sacks down to the town dump and chucked them in a dumpster.

Now the room's pretty bare and empty, which is just the way I like it. Bed, wardrobe, mirror. Books lined up along the bookshelf on the wall. Table and chair. And that's about it. Plain white walls. No pictures, no posters, no ornaments. Nice and clean. Functional.

I closed my eyes. I put my hands to my face and pressed my fingers to my eyelids and watched patterns emerge in the pure sightless black. Dazzling checkerboards of Day-Glo red and electric blue. Bright white bars of light, flashes, sparkles, fluorescent stars. Strange geometries of color — purple pyramids, earth-red squares, and flat lilac fields. There were even things that were colored with colors I'd never seen before. Nameless colors. It was too much. I took my hands from my eyes and stared blindly at the ceiling. After a minute or two the colors and patterns faded and my sight returned.

My eyes hurt.

I turned my thoughts to the next day. Dean was due at noon to collect his money. I wondered what he was thinking about now. Was he confident? Excited? Worried? Scared? Did he think he had it all worked out? Did he think it was going to be easy? Like taking candy from a baby?

Dean, Dean, Dean . . . don't you know that babies bite?

The telephone rang.

I jumped off the bed, ran down the stairs, and grabbed at the receiver.

"Hello!"

"Martyn?"

"Alex!"

"Are you all right? You sound like you're out of breath."

"I was upstairs," I said, trying to calm down. "Where've you been?"

"Out with Mom. Sorry, I meant to tell you yesterday. I forgot."

She wasn't out with her mom this morning. "Where d'you go?" I asked her.

"Mary's. You know, her friend from the hospital, the one with the horses."

Horses? "Oh, right."

"Anyway —"

"Are you coming over?"

She didn't answer. I heard muffled voices in the background. "Alex?"

"Sorry, Martyn. Mom was talking to me. What did you say?"

"Are you coming over?" I repeated.

She hesitated, then spoke in a whisper. "I'd better not. Mom's a bit suspicious about the car. I'd better stay in."

"What?" I said. "What about the car?"

"Nothing really, little things. I forgot to readjust the seat, the gas was low."

"What did she say?"

"She didn't *say* anything. She just mentioned it and gave me a funny look. Don't worry about it."

"Yeah, but —"

"Don't *worry*," she said. "It's nothing. I just think it'd be a good idea if I stayed in tonight, you know, just to be on the safe side."

"I suppose so. . . ."

"It's late, anyway."

"Is it?"

"It's past eleven."

"Oh."

"I'll come over first thing tomorrow."

"OK."

"All right?"

"Yeah, OK."

"I'll see you then, then."

"First thing?"

"First thing."

"OK."

"I'd better go, Martyn. I'll see you tomorrow."

"'Bye."

Click.

You wait all day for something, then when it finally comes you wish you hadn't bothered.

I gave up on Sunday and went to bed.

I was too tired to sleep. All I could do was lie there staring into the darkness, and it wasn't long before the emptiness began tingling at the back of my eyes. I suppose I could have stayed there and soaked it all up, or let it all out some more, but I just couldn't face it. So I got up and put the light on. I took *The Big Sleep* off the bookshelf and sat up reading until my eyes were so heavy I couldn't make out the words anymore. For a while I just lay back half-dreaming — detectives in powder-blue suits, generals in wheelchairs, tropical orchids, men in Chinese coats and naked girls with long jade earrings — until at last my mind switched off and I fell asleep with my head resting on the open book.

MONDAY

Sometimes I try to imagine what happens when I'm sleeping. You can never know, can you? You never see yourself asleep. You don't know what happens. You lose yourself. Every night, you lose yourself to an unknown world.

I imagine the structure of my body idling. Ticking over. The innards at rest. I'm automatic. Electric things that work me continue to work, crackling in the dead dark of my head. I move, crawling blindly on twisted sheets, twitching. I talk to myself about things I don't understand and I watch talking pictures, broken images, rummages of life's trash. Dreams. The Sleeping Me. A self-cleansing organism, scraping out the useless muck of a mind. Washing up.

As I sleep, the room is quiet. Pipes inside the walls hum unheard, the clock barely ticks. The bathroom faucet drips soft and slow, discoloring the green bath mat.

And outside, the night sky is big and magnificent. Beneath its pure black dome, the trappings of the street shrink to nothing. Toys of cars, little squares of bricks, gray lines. Unseen blobs of skin and bone. Tiny things under the moon. A white moth fluttering in the night air. Something small slithering in the rustle of dead leaves under a bush. A stunted tree, bent and motionless in the glare of a streetlight.

And I just lie there sleeping.

Something must see it all.

I woke early and lay in bed for a while listening to the sounds of the morning. The rattle and hum of the milk truck working its way down the street, clinking bottles, the milkman whistling. Small birds cursing at the snow. Someone, somewhere, was shouting at a dog. *Murphy! Murphy! Murphy! MURPHY!* The dog was called Murphy. Then, a little later, mailman sounds: footsteps, mail slots flapping, more whistling.

Why do they always whistle?

I tried it myself as I got out of bed and dressed. Whistling a nonsense tune, I pulled on jeans, T-shirt, shirt, sweater, and two pairs of socks. It was icy cold. Nice and icy.

Whistling. I got it. Whistling — it makes you feel better. It takes your mind off what you're doing, but at the same time, helps you concentrate. Like chewing gum.

I whistled into the bathroom and whistled as I whistled. Then I whistled downstairs, whistled through the mail, and whistled as I threw it all in the trash. I turned on the radio, retuned to Radio 2, and whistled along with the music while I boiled some eggs.

I seemed to have developed a craving for boiled eggs.

Through the kitchen window low gray skies threatened more snow. I dipped toast into my egg and spooned it into my mouth. Birds huddled together on the wall, fluffed up fat against the cold, their dark little bodies outlined starkly against the still-white streaks of hard-packed snow. A pigeon with only half a tail landed clumsily on the wall and the smaller birds fluttered into the air, then settled again. The pigeon waddled along the wall looking lost. I wondered what had happened to its tail. A cat? Dog? Air rifle?

I killed a bird once. When I was a little kid. Shot it dead. I had this little air gun. I don't remember where I got it from. Maybe I swapped it for something? Anyway, it wasn't a very good one. Not very powerful. I'd been popping away at garden birds for weeks without ever hitting anything. Sparrows, starlings, blackbirds, they just sat there on the fence, or on the roofs of houses, watching nonchalantly as I took aim from my bedroom window, fired, and missed. They were too far away. The pellets headed off in the right direction but ran out of steam halfway there and nose-dived into the ground. I had to get closer. Or make the birds come closer to me. So I made this stupid little bird table. Just a flat board nailed to a stick, really. I stuck it in the ground right below the bedroom window, piled sliced bread on top, then went back upstairs and waited, loaded gun in hand. After a minute or two, a sparrow landed. The flimsy bird table wobbled slightly then steadied. I took aim. The sparrow was nice and close. I could see his hard little beak, his small black eyes. I pulled the trigger, the pistol spat, and the sparrow fell. Just like that. I stared in disbelief. I'd killed it. Stopped its life. Shot it dead. Just pulled the trigger and shot it dead. I can still see it now, a small bundle of limp feathers, neck broken, a pearl of bright red blood on its beak. Limp and heartless.

It left me cold. Ashamed. Scared. Dirty and bad.

But at the same time I felt something else, too. Something not all bad. I don't know. A sense of power, maybe. Control. Strength. Something like that. Whatever it was, it was too confusing. I was too young to understand. I didn't want to understand. So I ran downstairs, out into the garden, checked to see that no one was watching, picked up the dead bird by the tip of a wing, and threw it into the trash can. Gone. Out of sight. It didn't happen. Forget it.

I didn't forget it.

The half-tailed pigeon was gone now; the wall outside the window was birdless. Next-door's cat was padding along the wall, high-stepping through the snow, a smug furry grin on its face. I don't like cats. Especially that one. Fat little creep. I banged on the window and it scampered.

Alex seemed a little distracted when she arrived. I studied her face as she removed her fur hat and hung up her coat. The way she moved her lips, the shape of her mouth, her eyes — distracted or not, I could watch her forever. She wiped at her brow with a finger, half-smiled, then adjusted the ribbon in her hair. It was a black one today, as black as her hair. Her faded denim shirt was black, too, worn loose over tight black jeans. Framed in black, the pale oval of her face shone with perfect simplicity. Like a china doll's.

"What?" she said.

I was staring. "Nothing. Sorry."

She gazed down at the floor, licking her lips, as if she wanted to say something but couldn't remember what it was. I waited.

Then, to my surprise, she looked up at me with a sparkling smile, reached over, and kissed me on the cheek.

"Sorry, Martyn."

"What for?" I said.

"Yesterday. For not coming over." She hesitated. "I just needed to get away from it all for a while."

"From what?"

"Everything. Your dad. Dean. You. I mean, this whole situation . . . it's pretty crazy. We disposed of a *body*, for God's sake. And now, today . . ."

"But we talked about that —"

"I *know* we did. I'm not saying I've changed my mind, I'm not backing out or anything. I just needed some time away from it. That's all." She touched my arm. "I'm just telling you why I didn't come around yesterday, why I didn't call."

I nodded. I didn't know what to say.

After a moment she took her hand away.

"OK?" she said.

"Yeah."

"Good."

"Right. What's the time?"

She looked at her watch. "Ten o'clock."

"We've got two hours before Dean gets here. Let's go over it again."

We went over it again.

Afterward, over tea and toast, I brought up the subject of money.

"I've been thinking about it," I told her. "We don't *have* to wait for the check to clear before we start spending. We could go into town this afternoon."

"But the check won't clear until tomorrow," Alex argued. "You won't be able to get any cash out until then."

"Who said anything about cash?"

"What do you mean?"

"I've got a checkbook. I could buy stuff with checks. I can forge Dad's signature."

"But —"

"Look, I'll show you. Hold on." I went upstairs and got Dad's bank card from the bureau, and a pen and piece of paper.

"I was always signing things in his name," I explained as I dashed off a series of signatures. "Delivery notes, letters to Social Security, prescriptions . . . it's easy. See?" I showed her my forged signatures, then the real one on the back of the bank card. "You can't tell the difference, can you?"

I did another one. *W. PIG.* A big droopy W, a dot, then a pathetic *PIG*, three scrunched up little capital letters that looked as if they were written by a six-year-old. A six-year-old with a broken hand. "You've got to do it quick," I said, showing her again. "If you start to think about it, you lose it."

"That's very good, Martyn."

"Thank you."

"The only thing is —"

"What?"

"Who's going to take a check from a fourteen-year-old boy?"

I stopped signing and looked at her. "The man at the off-licence always does. He even lets me sign them in Dad's name."

"Well he would, wouldn't he?"

"I don't see why —"

"Yes, you do."

I paused, looking at her.

"Come on, Martyn," she said. "Don't be stupid. Even if someone *did* take a check — not that they would — but even if they did, checks are traceable. Checks are dangerous. Just wait until tomorrow, wait for the check to clear, then use the bank card. One more day isn't going to hurt, is it? Stick to the plan."

She was right, of course. It was a stupid idea, embarrassingly stupid. I wished there was a hole I could sink into.

I tried a grin. "What would I do without you?"

"You'd think of something." She smiled, then stood up. "I have to go to the bathroom. Give me the bank card and I'll put it back in the bureau." I passed her the card. She picked up the paper with the forged signatures on. "You don't want to leave this lying around, do you? I'll flush it."

"Thanks, Alex," I said. "For everything."

She looked at me and laughed.

I smiled. "What? What's so funny?"

"Nothing," she said, controlling herself, "nothing's funny."

It bothered me sometimes, the way she changed. One second this; the next second that. It was hard to keep up. But then we all have our odd little ways, I suppose.

At eleven o'clock I walked her to the bus stop. The dark sky looked as if it had never been anything else but dark. Icy winds whipped through the alleyways between houses, scattering ragged arcs of loose snow across the road.

Dean was due in an hour.

"What time will he leave his apartment?" I asked.

"Probably about eleven thirty, eleven forty-five."

"You've got the key?"

She nodded, patting her pocket. "It was funny, really, when

he gave it to me. It was as if he thought it was a really *loving* thing to do, you know, like he was asking me to marry him or something. I think he expected me to swoon."

"Did you?"

"All he really wanted was someone to clean up his apartment while he was at work."

The bus shelter offered little protection against the wind. We sat shivering on the folding seats. Alex clutched her bag close to her body, staring straight ahead.

"It'll be all right," I said.

"Yeah."

We sat in silence. There was nothing else to say.

Five days ago we'd sat here. The picture was clear in my mind. Wednesday. Alex waiting for the bus, going to Dean's. Me with bags full of Christmas shopping and a runny nose. Alex making fun of the turkey, leaning over and peering into the shopping bags, nudging one with a foot.

Nice-looking chicken.

It's a turkey.

Bit small for a turkey.

It's a small turkey.

I think you'll find that's a chicken, Martyn.

Grinning at each other. Her eyes shining in the gloom of the bus shelter, like marbles, clear and round and perfect. Just sitting there, chatting, doing nothing, watching the world go by —

"Here's the bus," she said, digging in her bag for her purse.

Was that then, or now?

The bus pulled in and the doors *pished* open. Alex stepped on. I watched her pay. I watched the bus driver click buttons on his ticket machine. I watched the bus ticket snicker out. I watched the way her eyes blinked slowly and I watched her mouth say *Thank you* and I watched the coal-black shine of her hair as she took the bus ticket and rolled it into a tube and stuck it in the corner of her mouth and walked gracefully to the back of the bus. And I watched and waited in vain for her to turn her head as the bus lurched out into the street and shuddered up the road and disappeared around the corner.

She didn't look back.

Back home I tidied up. Without Dad around the place was easy to keep clean. I used to hate the mess he made. Stuff all over the floor, dirty plates and cups, glasses, bottles, newspapers, cigarette ash, clothes, shoes — it was a tip. As soon as I'd cleared it all away there'd be more. A never-ending supply of garbage. I couldn't stand it. All that jumble and dirt; it made me so I couldn't think straight. I need to see clean surfaces, flat and uncluttered. I need to see the true shape of things, the lines, the angles. Mess messes me up. Dad couldn't care less. He'd just sit there in his armchair, surrounded by his own debris, smoking and drinking, happy as a clam. Not a care in the world. Lord Muck. King of the Dump. Sometimes I think he did it on purpose. Messed the place up just to annoy me. He enjoyed it. Thought it was funny.

Now, although I couldn't do anything about its overall shabbiness, the house was as clean as a whistle. Clean and clear. No mess. No garbage. No debris. Clean floor, clean kitchen, clean tables, clean everything. Clean and staying clean. And it was a pleasure to keep clean. There was nothing to it. Strolling around, dusting here and there, pecking a stray piece of cotton from the carpet, adjusting the couch cushions. Whistling as I worked.

When I was done, satisfied that everything was spick-and-span, I settled down in the armchair to wait for Dean.

Calm, relaxed, my head unjumbled.

I was ready.

Five minutes later I heard the faint insect buzz of Dean's motorcycle. Down at the bottom of the main road — *bzzzzz* — around the turn — *bzbzzzz* — up the hill — *bzzzzzz* — the high-pitched whine getting louder and more desperate as it struggled up past the church, then — *nnn-nnn-nnn-nnn* — changing gear and slowing to take the corner into the street — *bzbzbzzzz* — closer and louder — *BZZZZZ* — like a giant wasp inside a tin can — *ZZZZZZ* — and then — *ZZZZzzz chugga chugga chugga* — as it slowed to a halt and parked across the road. The engine revved uselessly a couple of times and then died.

Silence.

Through the window I watched the black globe of Dean's helmet bobbing across the street. I listened to the clump of his boots as he mounted the pavement and stopped outside the door.

The doorbell rang.

I didn't move.

It rang again, longer this time.

I let it ring, then rose slowly from the chair and went out into the hall. Dean's dark figure loomed behind the door, his bulbous black head and lame body twisted out of shape by the molded glass, like some kind of thin-legged, long-armed, dome-headed alien.

I stepped forward and opened the door. "Yes?"

He glared down at me for a second, eyes hidden behind the dark visor of his helmet, then strode past me into the hall. I shut the door.

"Wha Alf?" he said, struggling with the straps of his helmet.

"What?"

He pulled the helmet off his head. "Where's Alex?" he repeated, smoothing his ponytail.

I shrugged. "She's not here. Does it matter?"

"No." He sniffed. "You on your own, then?"

"No."

He peered into the kitchen. "Who else is here?"

"You."

Watery eyes stared down at me. "You think you're funny?"

"Funnier than you."

He curled his lip, trying to look hard. It didn't work. He wouldn't look hard if he was dipped in concrete. His ill-fitting black leather jacket and black leather pants looked as if they belonged to someone else. The skin of his face was loose and sheenless, pale and puffy from long hours gaping at a computer screen, like a lump of raw dough. Doughboy.

Standing there like a lummox, he lit a cigarette and blew smoke in my direction.

"You can put that down if you want," I said, nodding at the helmet dangling from his hand.

He almost said thanks, then remembered he was supposed to be hard, so he sneered and dropped the helmet on the hall table.

What had Alex ever seen in him? I thought. How could she . . . with that?

"Do you miss her?" I asked suddenly.

"Who? Alex?" He laughed coldly. "Miss her? I'm glad to see the back of her. Snotty little witch. There's plenty more where that came from." He stroked his ponytail and smirked. "Why? Looking for your chance, then, Pigman?"

"Alex is just a friend."

"Yeah?"

"You wouldn't understand."

He puffed on his cigarette. "She's too much for you, I know that. Too much of a woman. Know what I mean?"

"She's just a friend."

"I'd stick to someone your own age if I were you. Kissing behind the bike sheds, that kind of stuff. *Kid's* stuff. Alex, she's something else." He winked. "She'd wear you out."

Idiot.

I went into the front room and sat down in the armchair. Dean followed hesitantly, cautiously examining the room as he entered.

"Where is it?" he said.

"What?"

"You know what."

"The body?"

He nodded.

"Gone," I said.

He said nothing. Standing in the middle of the room, fiddling with the zippers on his jacket, smoking his cigarette, unsure how to react.

"Sit down," I said, indicating the couch.

The cushions slouched forward as he sat down and he had to grab the armrest and cross his legs to avoid sliding off. He flicked his ponytail to one side and tapped cigarette ash on the floor in a futile attempt to regain his poise. He was a useless slob. A sad human being, hardly worthy of the name. Six feet of wet dough.

"Well?" I said.

"What?"

"Did you bring the tapes?"

"Have you got the money?"

"Show me the tapes."

"Show me the money."

I glanced out of the window. Sparse snow was falling gently, drifting leisurely in the air. *Big, fat, lazy flakes, fluttering, see-sawing, circling, taking their time, riding down slowly through the cold thickness of the air. Soft white crystals . . .*

"You're not getting any money," I said.

He opened his mouth, then shut it again. He sniffed and rubbed at his mouth. "What?"

"You're not getting any money."

"Why not?"

"Because it's mine."

We stared at each other. His eyes were blank. I could see right down into his soul; there was nothing there. He sucked hard on his cigarette, blinked, then jerked the cigarette from his mouth and blew out a long stream of smoke that drifted up to the ceiling and settled in a blue-gray cloud. Tough guy.

I waited, still staring. It's your move, Dean. What are you going to do? Better make up your mind. You can't just sit there smoking cigarettes.

He fumbled in the pocket of his leather jacket, pulled out the mini-cassette, and flourished it like a conjuror's rabbit.

"What about *this*?" he said.

"What about it?"

He paused, looking puzzled.

I smiled.

He tried again. "No money, no tape."

I carried on smiling.

"Do you understand, Pig? No money, no tape. If I don't get the money, this —" he tapped the tape, "this goes to the police."

"I don't think so."

"No?"

"No."

"Don't think I won't."

"You won't."

"No?"

"No."

"Why not?"

I stood up and crossed to the window. The road outside was thinly covered with fresh white snow, like a layer of frosting on a cake. Dean's motorcycle leaned on its kickstand across the street, an ugly-looking thing covered in chrome with a puke-green gas tank that bulged out at the sides. It looked cheap and nasty, like a toy from the Bargain Bin. A toy motorcycle for a toy man. I turned and looked at him. Crouched awkwardly on the couch he looked shrunken and pathetic.

"Do you know what forensics is?" I asked him.

He frowned. "Forensics? It's fingerprints, blood, stuff like that. What's that got to do with anything?"

I crossed the room and stopped behind the couch, looking

down at the top of his head. He swiveled around and watched, perplexed, as I reached down and plucked a long blond hair from the back of the couch. Dangling the hair from my fingers, I held it up to the light. "You'll be bald in a few years' time."

"What?"

"Look," I said, pointing to the back of the couch. "Loose hairs all over the place. It's disgusting."

His hand moved automatically to his beloved ponytail. "What are you talking about?"

"Do you want to know what we did with the body?"

He shook his head, confused.

"I'll tell you. We wrapped it in a sleeping bag, weighed it down with rocks, and dropped it in a gravel pit out at the old quarry." I paused to let that sink in, then picked another loose hair from the back of the couch and began twisting it around my finger. "Last time you were here you dropped hair all over the place. All over the kitchen floor. After you left I picked them all up. But I didn't throw them away. What I did, before we wrapped Dad's body in the sleeping bag, I stuck some of the hairs under his fingernails. Wound them around his fingers. Your hairs, Dean. Do you see? Do you know what I mean?"

Vacant eyes looked back at me.

I went on. "And a cigarette butt, too. Remember? You dropped one on the kitchen floor. That went in the sleeping bag as well. Hairs and a cigarette butt. Your hairs, your cigarette butt. It's amazing what the police can do these days. Hairs, cigarette butts, fingerprints, DNA. Forensics, it's amazing stuff."

Dean watched me as I moved back to the armchair and sat down, his mouth and left eyelid twitching in nervous unison.

"Do you understand?" I said.

He shook his head slowly. "You're lying."

"No."

He was paler than a dead fish. "I don't believe it."

I shrugged.

"Prove it."

"I can't." I smiled. "You'll just have to trust me."

"What if I don't?"

"That's up to you. It's your choice. If you want to take the chance. . . ."

"Bastard."

"If the body's found — which it will be if anyone hears the tape, I'll make sure of that — there's enough evidence there to put you away for murder. More than enough."

"But the tape —"

"Implicates me and Alex, too. I know. Think about it, though. She's a young girl, I'm a kid. We're innocents. You forced us into it, Dean, you *made* us help you. Even if we *were* convicted, which is highly unlikely, the worst we'd get is a year or two in some kind of detention center, if that. But you, you'll go to prison, whatever happens. Real prison. Not some kids' holiday home run by social workers. Prison. Locked up, twenty-four hours a day, for the rest of your life. With *real* bad guys. Murderers, rapists, perverts . . . think about it, Dean. Life. It's a long time."

He stared at the floor, unconsciously rubbing at his eye. "They wouldn't believe it," he said half-heartedly. "Why would I kill your old man?"

"For the money."

"I didn't know anything about the money!"

"Alex told you."

"She didn't!"

"Can you prove it?"

He couldn't answer. He just sat there, deflated. Lost. There was no way out. I had him. He couldn't afford *not* to believe it.

"The tape," I demanded, holding out my hand.

"I've got copies."

I shook my head. "You haven't."

"What?"

"Alex has got them."

"How? When?"

I glanced at the clock. "About fifteen minutes ago. You gave her a key to your apartment, remember? That's where she's been while you've been here. Searching your apartment, looking for copies of the tape. We knew you wouldn't bring them here."

"She's been in my apartment?"

"You gave her a key."

"Witch! I'll kill her!" His eyes were cold and furious and I thought for a moment he was about to go for me. I braced myself, but his fury quickly faded. He was nothing. Less than nothing, now. Beaten, lost, humiliated, he sat there like a baby — a six-foot-tall baby dressed in black leather. Helpless, clueless, weak, white, and flabby. A gentle breeze would have blown him over. I reached over and took the tape from his hand. Candy from a baby.

I went over and stood at the window. A trail of footprints led across the street, stark and fresh in the snow, heading toward Dean's motorcycle. Or away from it, I couldn't tell. Some kid, I thought, taking a look at the bike.

The snow fell steadily. I looked up into the tumbling white sky and picked out a single snowflake. It seemed to fall much more slowly than all the other flakes, as if it didn't want to land. It wanted to fall forever. And as I stood there watching it come down I somehow felt myself becoming part of it. I know it sounds ridiculous, but I swear it's true. There was me, Martyn Pig, standing at the window looking up at the sky; and there was another me, a star-shaped me, drifting down in the snow. I could feel the cold air breezing through my fingers. I was crystal. Strong and intricate and beautiful. I was weightless. Floating. Far above the ground. I could see for miles. I could see the gray clutter of town, the factories, the winding brown river, the distant roads and cars, the houses, roofs, the street below, a gawky-looking kid gazing up through a window . . . and although I was just one of a million tiny jewels of ice, there was only me. All I had to do was fall, and that's what I was doing. Free and easy, no fear, no feeling at all, just falling gently through the afternoon air to land without a sound on the snow-covered roof of a Buick. And then I started to fade away. Just before the darkness descended, I looked over at the boy in the window. He looked back at me, ran his fingers through his hair, and then turned away.

Dean was just sitting there, staring at the wall. "I thought you'd gone," I said.

He rose and left without a word. I heard the front door open, then quietly close. I watched from the window as he crossed the street, head down, shoulders stooped, his black garb dotted white with snow. I watched as he pulled down the visor of his helmet, mounted his motorcycle and wearily kicked it into life. There was no revving, this time, no angry buzzing. He just drove off cautiously, turned the corner, and was gone. The shining black tire tracks immediately began to fill with snow.

I listened to the sound of the motorcycle as it picked up speed, heading down the steep hill of the main road toward the turn, fading into the distance. And then, quite suddenly, it was gone. One second, a faint waspish whining; the next second, nothing.

Gone.

Odd, I thought.

I shrugged. It'll be the snow, some kind of acoustic illusion.

Acoustic illusion? Is there such a thing?

It doesn't matter.

You did it.

Perfect. Plan A. Smooth as you like. No problems. All settled. Dad gone, Dean gone. Nice and neat. I smiled.

All that's left is me and Alex. And sixty thousand dollars.

Sweet.

Ten minutes later Alex was at the door.

"That was quick."

She didn't answer.

"Did you get the tapes?"

She didn't even look at me, just walked straight past into the front room and squatted down in front of the fire, warming her hands. I followed. There was a glazed look in her eyes, distant, not-quite-there. Her movements were strange, too. Slow and stiff, like a sleepwalker. She started rubbing her hands together, over and over again, rubbing, rubbing, rubbing. I noticed the thumb and two fingers of her right hand were smeared with something black.

"Alex?"

She didn't seem to hear me.

Somewhere in the distance a siren wailed. Ambulance. Alex was motionless. Staring, her hands clasped tightly together, listening to the siren approach. Down the main road it came, closer, louder — a harsh wailing sound. The siren tone shifted as the ambulance passed by and then it faded. Alex murmured something under her breath and then began rubbing her hands again.

"Alex?" I said quietly.

She didn't reply.

I reached down and touched her shoulder. "Alex?"

Her hands stopped rubbing and she looked up, surprised to see me.

"Martyn."

"Are you all right?"

She blinked. Her eyes suddenly cleared and she stood up and kissed me with ice-cold lips. It felt a bit weird, to be honest. Like she was someone else.

"Excuse me," she said, and left the room.

I heard her climb the stairs and go into the bathroom. Almost immediately the faucet started running and the toilet flushed. Sick again, I thought. Shock, probably. That's all it is. A bit of shock. Aftershock. Sneaking into Dean's apartment, poking around inside, on her own, it must have scared her. She's frightened, that's all. Nothing to worry about.

I sat and waited, gazing out of the window at the snow. I was starting to get sick of the sight of it.

• • •

When Alex came down ten minutes later it was as if nothing had happened. She was herself again. Smiling, bright and breezy, fresh. Clean.

"So," she said, settling into the couch, "what did he say?"

"Who?"

"Dean, stupid. Who else? What did he say?"

"Not much. There wasn't much he could say, really."

"I wish I'd been here to see his face."

I told her all about it, from the moment he arrived to the moment I watched him leave. Except for the stuff about me and her, I left that out. And the thing with the snow. She listened eagerly, perched on the edge of the couch, staring at me with her big brown eyes.

"What did he say when you told him I was in his apartment?" she asked.

"He wasn't too pleased," I said. "He called you a few choice names."

Something flashed across her face and then, in an instant, it was gone. She smiled and shrugged her shoulders. "Well, sticks and stones . . ."

"How did it go, in the apartment?" I asked.

"Easy, no problem. I just walked in, got what I wanted, and left."

"You got the tapes?"

She reached into her bag and pulled out the mini-taperecorder and a box of cassettes. "I checked them all on the way back. He only made one copy. Idiot. He actually *labeled* it, look." She held out the tape for me to see. It was labeled on the back: *A & MP, talk, copy*.

I laughed. "Dean, the master criminal."

"Mister Big," added Alex.

"Not so big now."

She smiled.

It was all so easy. It was perfect. Everything had worked. I felt good inside. I'd set out to do something and I'd done it. Me. My plan. My idea. I was proud of myself.

"Do you think we'll see him again?" I asked.

She looked away, but not before I saw that funny look cross her face once more. It was like a face beneath a mask, revealed for an instant, then gone again. Too quick to recognize.

"No," she said softly, "I don't think we'll see Dean again."

Late afternoon. The Scrabble board was almost full. Alex was sitting with her elbows on the table, head cupped in her hands, staring at her letters. She never moved them around in the rack, just stared at them, with the tip of her tongue poking out between her lips, concentrating, waiting for a word to appear.

We'd checked through all Dean's tapes again, just to make sure, but there was nothing of interest on any of them. The original and the copy of the blackmail tape we'd burned in a metal bucket. I'd put the burnt remains along with the tape recorder and all the other tapes in a shopping bag, topped it up with kitchen garbage, then nipped out and stuffed it into a trash can outside someone else's house a couple of streets away.

Now, sipping tea, staring out into the afternoon darkness, I was thinking about tomorrow. The Plan. Part 2. There wasn't much to it, really. Alex would come over in the morning, we'd go into town, draw out five hundred and fifty dollars, and get spending. The only thing was . . . we hadn't really talked about what we were going to spend it *on*. I felt a bit awkward about it, to be honest. I didn't want to appear too pushy, you know, too forward. But then I didn't want Alex to think I wasn't prepared to do whatever she wanted, either. If she wanted to spend the money on presents, clothes, that kind of stuff . . . well, that was fine. As far as it went. But what I really wanted was to get out of here. I wasn't expecting us to just jet off somewhere immediately, but a trip to the travel agent would be a start. They might have something on short notice, a country cottage in Scotland or Wales, something like that. We could get on a train, maybe even take the car. Anywhere would do. Anywhere but here.

But, as I said, I didn't really know how to bring it up.

"We'd better start early tomorrow," I said. "It's Christmas Eve, places shut early."

"Hmm?" she said, without looking up from her letters.

"Tomorrow. It's Christmas Eve. Places shut early."

"No they don't."

"Some do."

"Like what?"

"I don't know. Banks, travel age —"

"But we don't need a bank, do we?" she smiled. "Just a cash machine. Cash machines don't close."

"No, I suppose not."

She went back to staring at her letters.

What we could do, I thought, if she didn't want to go anywhere right away, we could go to the travel agent just for a look, maybe get some brochures, find out how much things cost, then spend the money on presents and stuff and have a nice quiet Christmas here. I don't suppose another day or two would hurt. I could get some really expensive food in, cook us something tasty. Maybe hang around for a couple of days. It'd give us enough time to get a load of money together, and then after Christmas we could really go somewhere.

"You could come here for dinner, if you like," I suggested. "Bring your mom."

She looked up. "What?"

"You and your mom, I'll cook you a Christmas dinner."

"Yeah, OK."

"She's not a vegetarian or anything is she?"

"Who?"

"Your mom."

"Why should she be?"

"I don't know. I was just asking. What do you prefer, chicken or turkey?"

"Anything, really, it doesn't matter. We're not fussy. As long as it's not that horrible thing you got from the market." She grinned. "Now, let me concentrate on these letters."

After a minute or two of silence, she went to put a word down, then changed her mind. I smiled to myself. When we'd first started playing Scrabble together it used to really annoy me how slow she was. Unbelievably slow. Sometimes she'll take as long as five minutes before putting down a word. Then, when she does finally play it, it's something stupid like CAT or IT. But I'm used to it now. I don't mind. I just like to watch her play.

"What do you normally do?" I said.

"What?"

"For Christmas. What do you normally do?"

"Nothing much."

She started tapping a finger lightly on the table. *Tap tap tap.*

Meaning: Shut up, Martyn, I'm trying to think of a word. So I shut up and looked out of the window. Nothing but darkness and snow. I looked at Alex. Staring. Thinking. I tried to imagine what she'd look like when she was old. But I couldn't do it. It was a face that could only ever be young. Me, I could see myself as an old man. Short and bony, bald, covered in moles, face caved in. I'd be a miserable old coot, always moaning, waving my cane in people's faces — *Get out of the way, can't you see I'm old*? I'd have bad teeth and a permanent dribble stain on my chin and I'd wear the same clothes *all* the time —

"Sag," said Alex.

That was her word. SAG.

Tapping each letter with a fingertip, she added up the score, marked it on the score pad, reached for the letter bag, closed her eyes and drew out two more letters, placed them in her letter tray, and immediately commenced staring. That's how she plays. Lost in her own little world. It never ceased to amaze me.

I looked at my letters. A, C, H, T, J, I, H. I thought for a moment, then added a word. AITCH, the A tagged onto the bottom of SAG making SAGA.

Alex glanced up. "Aitch? What's that?"

"Aitch," I said, taking the last five letters from the bag. "The letter H. Aitch. As in H_2O."

"That's not a word."

"Of course it is."

"Is it?"

"Yes."

"I thought it was haitch."

I laughed.

"What?" she scowled.

"Nothing. It's aitch. A-I-T-C-H. Aitch. Trust me."

She glared at me for a moment, shook her head, then went back to her letter-staring. She couldn't win. I was already about 100 points ahead and there were no letters left. The game was almost over. She never wins, but it doesn't seem to bother her. She always concentrates right up to the end, taking ages over each word, thinking things through, not making her move until she's absolutely sure. And that's probably what was worrying me about bringing up the idea of going away together. She'd want to think it through. She'd want to weigh up the options, decide what was best. She'd want to make sure it wasn't a mistake. Anyway, I knew I'd have to say something soon. It wouldn't wait for ever.

What's wrong with now?

Now?

It's as good a time as any. You said it yourself — it's no good wishing things were different, wishing you could turn the clock back, wishing you had another chance, because things aren't different, you can't turn the clock back, you don't get another chance. The only thing to do is say to yourself: What's the worst that can happen? And then do it.

Right. What's the worst that can happen?

Go on, then. Just open your mouth and say it.

I took a deep breath. "We could be out of here by Christmas Day."

Alex didn't move. I thought for a moment she hadn't heard me. Then she raised her head and looked me in the eye. "What?"

"We could go somewhere," I said. "Just jump on a train, anywhere you like."

"What do you mean?"

I cleared my throat. "You and me, you know. We could go away somewhere."

"A vacation?"

I shrugged. "Yeah . . . a vacation. Or maybe —"

"Me and you?"

"Why not?"

"When?"

"Now, tomorrow, after Christmas. Whenever you like."

She didn't say anything, just stared at me, gazing deep into my eyes. I couldn't stand it. I had to look away. I looked down at the letters in my rack. H, U, J, S, A, D, T. Stupid little words jumped out at me. SAD. Come on, Alex. HAT. Say something. HUT. Anything. SHUT. Yes. DUST. No. DASH. Anything. JUST. Don't laugh. . . .

"Let's talk about it tomorrow," she said eventually.

I looked up. "It's Christmas Eve tomorrow."

"I know."

"We don't want to leave it too late. Things'll get booked up."

"I know. Let me think about it, all right?" She stood up. "Look, I have to go now. I promised Mom I'd help her prepare for her audition."

"But —"

"We'll sort it out tomorrow."

"Anywhere," I repeated. "Anywhere you like."

"I *know*, Martyn. I know. Anywhere. I said I'd think about it. OK?"

"OK."

We'd talk about it tomorrow.

• • •

She kissed me again before she left. Just a peck on the cheek, and then she was gone. I watched her cross the empty street and follow the pavement down toward her house, a slight dark figure stooped against the falling snow. The touch of her kiss on my cheek grew colder with every step she took.

There she goes, I thought. Just an unknown shape of a girl disappearing into a shroud of snow.

Did I ever know her?

I stood in the doorway for a while, waiting, but she didn't look back.

She never looked back.

That was the last time I ever saw her.

TUESDAY

I wasn't that worried when she didn't show up the following morning. Not at first, anyway. Annoyed, maybe. But not worried. Alex was often late. She could never understand why it bothered me. "I'm here now, aren't I?" she'd say. She was right, in a way. If you like someone enough, it doesn't matter how long they keep you waiting — as long they turn up in the end, it's all right.

I can't help it, though. I hate waiting for someone to turn up. I can't understand why anyone should be late for anything. Unless something disastrous happens there's no reason for it. No reason at all. *I'm* never late for anything. I always make sure I'm early, then if something *does* happen, I've still got time to get wherever I'm going.

If I can do it, why can't everyone else?

It was Christmas Eve, I'd told her that. Places shut early. I wanted out of here. Now. Just go, get on a train, a boat, a plane, get on and go. Anywhere. I'd *told* her that.

It was nine-thirty. Where the hell was she?

I waited. Ten minutes, twenty minutes, half an hour. I rang her. No answer. I waited some more, pacing up and down, looking at the clock every two minutes. I rang again. No answer. I made some tea, I swore, I paced up and down some more. By ten-thirty I couldn't wait any longer. I put on my hat and coat and went over to her house.

A thick layer of snow covered the ground, crunching under my boots as I hurried down the road. The snow had stopped falling but it was still freezing cold. The street was gloomy and deserted. Darkly quiet. Heavy gray snow clouds hung low in the sky, covering everything in a cold, dark smog. The flat snow-crunch of my footsteps sounded bleak and lonely in the dull air.

The car was gone from outside her house. No tire tracks, so it must have left some time ago. I stood at the gate peering up at the windows. Curtains open, lights off, no movement. It looked empty. It felt empty. I knew it was empty. I stepped up and rang the bell, anyway. The distant ring had no effect. No footsteps, no doors opening, no muffled voices. I stepped to one side and looked in through the porch window. Nothing. Just an empty hallway, blurred through the patterned glass, and the vague shape of the kitchen doorway at the end of the hall, the door half-open, revealing a distorted triangle of black-and-white floor-tiles. Empty. As I stepped back my foot brushed against a milk bottle. The bottle wobbled and I reached down in time to stop it from toppling over. Two milk-bottles, both full. Unwanted.

There was no one home.

I turned back into the gloom.

Where was she? If she'd had to go somewhere, why hadn't she called? It was eleven o'clock now. Where the hell was she?

Halfway along the street I stopped and looked over my shoulder. I don't know what I was expecting to see. That dirty old VW Minibus turning the corner, Alex leaning out of the window, smiling and waving, calling out to me, Martyn! Hey, Martyn . . . but there was nothing there. And I could tell by the look of the street that there wasn't going to be anything there. It had a non-expectant look to it.

Maybe . . .

Maybe I was waiting in vain?

Maybe . . .

No.

She wouldn't do that. Don't even think about it.

I continued on home.

It's probably something stupid, I told myself. She'd had to go out with her mom, they'd had a fight, she'd forgotten to call me. Maybe the phone wasn't working? But then all she'd have to do was pop across the road and tell me. Two minutes. Or maybe they'd gone out earlier, shopping or something, visiting friends, and the car broke down? They could be stuck somewhere, stuck in the car. And she couldn't ring to let me know because there wasn't a phone nearby. Or perhaps they'd had an accident? The roads are bad, covered in ice. They're driving along somewhere, chatting, they take a corner too fast, slide off and smack into a hedge, or hit another car. . . . Yes, that could be it. An accident. They were in the hospital. That would explain it.

Believe it. It fits. It's a good solution. It explains everything.

Anything else, don't even think about it. Don't even think about it.

But as I entered the house and climbed the stairs I already

knew what I'd find. The truth has a way of shining through, no matter how hard you try to ignore it.

Dad's room felt cold and abandoned. Like a room that no one had ever lived in. I pulled back the curtains and opened the window but the air refused to come in. Pale morning shadows whispered memories into the void.

Staring eyes. Nothing like eyes. Mute, blind, unquestioning. Pale, bloodless, dead. Not dead, just sleeping.

Dad.

Are we bad?

Alex.

Look at her, look at that girl. Who else would do that for you?

I walked slowly across the room.

You'll have to close his eyes.

I opened the wardrobe.

Tell me what you want me to be and I'll be it.

Acting.

Anything: a situation, an emotion, a person, anything. I will act for you.

She was an actress.

Perfumed, made-up, artificial.

Her mom was an actress.

She can do anything: voices, the way people walk, their posture, anything. She's brilliant.

No jacket. There was no jacket in the wardrobe.

What are you doing? Nothing. Just putting his clothes away.

Gone.

I thought he was wearing his other one?

The brown one. Not the black one.

That's the jacket he was wearing, Martyn. I remember it. OK?

No, not OK.

She can do anything: voices, the way people walk, their posture, anything. She's brilliant.

Her bag.

A big old rucksacky thing with pockets and zippers all over the place, big enough to carry a small horse.

I went over to the bureau.

Just a bit queasy.

Opened it.

Would you mind going downstairs?

No checkbook, no bank card.

The roar of the toilet flushing. Taps running. Footsteps on the ceiling. What is she doing?

No birth certificate, no marriage certificate, no medical card. No lawyer's letters.

Give me the bank card and I'll put it back in the bureau.

How did she know?

Excuse me.

Why, Alex?

I'm not just a pretty face, you know.

Gone.

I'm not just a pretty face, you know.

Why?

I'm not just a pretty face, you know.

Why?

I'm not just a —

"SHUT UP!"

• • •

I walked downstairs in a daze and sank into the armchair, devastated. I couldn't believe it. I didn't believe it. Whatever it was, I didn't believe it. She wouldn't do that. Would she? She wouldn't. No, there must be a simple explanation. Think about it.

I thought about it.

Alex at the wardrobe. Tense and fidgety, eyes darting all over the room. Alex at the bureau. Reality. Laughter. Alex being sick. Poor Alex. Pretty Alex. Smart Alex . . . I thought about it until my head hurt, and then I thought about it some more — What about this? What about that? Yes? No? Maybe this. Maybe that. How? When? Why? What? Where? — but all it did was send me spinning around in circles. I couldn't think straight. It was like trying to get an octopus into a box: every time I got one leg in, another leg wriggled its way out. I wasn't getting anywhere. And then I remembered something Sherlock Holmes had said. *"When you have eliminated the impossible, whatever remains, however improbable, must be the truth."* So that's what I did. I made myself some tea, cleared my mind, then sat down and eliminated as much of the impossible as I could. And what I was left with was this: Alex took the checkbook, the bank card, Dad's identification, and the letters. She also took the jacket. And probably some other clothes, too. A shirt, a pair of pants, maybe a coat. Stuffed them all in that great bag of hers and just walked out. Why? Think about it . . . her mom. Of course! Her mom. She's about the same size as Dad, same age, same general appearance. She can act. Stick her in a dirty old shirt and jacket, some theatrical makeup . . . she's got ID . . . she dresses up as Dad, goes to the bank first thing this morning, and draws out the sixty thousand. No one's going to know the difference, especially a bank clerk. It's not impossible. Improbable? Maybe. But it's not impossible, is it?

Yes, it is.

It's impossible.

But then again. . . .

I don't know.

Maybe.

Yes.

No.

The octopus was getting out again. I was losing it. I even started thinking that it was all just a joke. A surprise. All right, supposing Alex *had* taken the checkbook and clothes and everything, that her mom *had* gone to the bank and drawn out all the money . . . it didn't necessarily mean they were cheating me, did it? Maybe they were just trying to *help*? To save me the bother of getting the money out bit by bit. After they'd got the sixty thousand dollars, Alex was going to turn up at the front door with a big smile on her face and a pocket full of cash — *ta daah!* But something had gone wrong. At the bank. Yes, that's it. Something went wrong at the bank. They got caught. That's where they are now, at the police station, being interrogated. . . .

Don't be stupid.

If Alex's mom had been arrested disguised as William Pig, carrying a checkbook and birth certificate in the name of William Pig, trying to draw out sixty thousand dollars from the account of William Pig, the police would have been around here hours ago. You don't need Inspector Morse to work that one out.

The truth.

Face it.

Whatever remains is the truth. They've gone. She's gone. Taken the money and gone. Ripped you off. Conned you. Used you. Betrayed you. It was all an act. She's an actress. How could you ever have thought anything else? You, Martyn Pig, with Alex? Beautiful Alex. No chance. Not in a million years. What have you got to offer? Dean was right. She's a woman. Know what I mean?

Dean. She was in it with Dean all along. Doughboy. Not as dumb as you thought. The two of them. They just used me to get Dad out of the way. . . .

No.

She wouldn't have let me frame him. If she was in it with Dean, she wouldn't have let me frame him.

No.

It was just her and her mom. Mother and daughter. Has-been and wannabe. I'd been had by a has-been and a wannabe.

Yes.

When?

When did she plan it? Right from the start? And whose idea was it? Her mom's? Or hers?

No.

How could she?

She couldn't.

No.

So, where's she gone?

Where is she?

What's she doing?

What am I going to do?

What *can* I do?

Did I ever mean *anything* to her?

Alex?

Answer me.

Tell me what happened.

Tell me what you've done.

Tell me it's impossible.

Tell me.

Please.

I was still sitting there at midnight when the doorbell rang.

Everything bad I'd thought about her disappeared in a flash. I
was wrong. I was stupid. I was an idiot. How could I ever have
thought she'd do such a thing? Betray me? Alex? We were
friends. Best friends. Maybe more. I raced to the door and flung
it open.

"We're looking for Mr. Pig."

The police. Two of them. The one who spoke was a silver-
haired man with a weathered face and sharp eyes. Medium
height, stout, round-shouldered. He had a crumpled look about
him. Beneath his raincoat he wore a dark blue suit that didn't
seem to fit properly.

"Mr. William Pig," he continued. "Is he in?"

I shook my head.

He held out his warrant card. "Detective Inspector Breece.
This is Detective Sergeant Finlay." Finlay flashed his card. Tall,
sad-faced, about thirty, he looked a bit dim but probably wasn't.
Breece looked past me into the hall. "Where's your dad, son?"

House lights clicked on across the street, bedroom curtains twitched.

Breece looked at me. "Are you on your own?"

I nodded again.

"What about your mom?"

I shook my head.

"Can you *speak*, son?"

"Yes," I said.

"What's your name?"

"Martyn," I said. *Martyn Pig. Martyn with a Y, Pig with an I and one G.*

"Where is he, Martyn?"

"Who?"

"Your father."

"I don't know."

He sighed. "Do you think we could come in?"

"What for?"

"Because it's bloody freezing out here, that's what for."

I hesitated. Breece just stood there waiting.

"Have you got a search warrant?" I asked him.

"A search warrant?"

I shrugged.

Breece sighed. "Look, Martyn. We just want to have a chat. About your dad. It won't take a minute."

I said nothing.

"If you want a search warrant," he continued in his deadpan voice, "Sergeant Finlay will wait here while I drive all the way back to the station. Then I'll have to wake someone up to sign the warrant. Then I'll have to drive all the way back and by the time I get here I'll be in a foul mood. Is that what you want?"

I didn't even know if they needed a search warrant. I'd only said it because I couldn't think of anything else to say.

What could I do? I stepped back and let them in.

Breece followed me into the kitchen and sat down at the table while I started to make some tea. I heard Finlay clomping up the stairs.

"Where's he going?"

"Bathroom," Breece answered.

I took three mugs from the cupboard and rinsed them in the sink. Breece's reflection shimmered in the kitchen window. He hadn't taken his raincoat off. His hair was wet. A notepad was open on the table.

"Do you know Dean West?" he said.

I nearly dropped a mug. "What?"

"Dean West," he repeated patiently. "Do you know him?"

"I thought you wanted to talk about my dad?"

"Just answer the question, please. Do you know Dean West?"

"Sort of."

"Sort of?"

"I know who he is."

Breece flipped through the pages of his notepad. "Tall, blond hair, ponytail? Rides a motorcycle."

"Could be."

"When did you last see him?"

The kettle boiled. I filled the mugs. "I don't really *know* him," I said. "He's a friend of a friend, you know."

Breece stared at my back. "When did you last see him?"

"I don't know. Months ago, in summer. In CVS."

"CVS?"

"The pharmacy."

"Not since then?"

I shook my head. "I don't think so, not that I can remember." Breece scribbled something in his notepad. "What's Dean got to do with anything?" I asked.

"That's what we're trying to find out."

Footsteps sounded from the stairs, then Finlay popped his head around the kitchen door. "Sir."

Breece rose and went out into the hall. He had a slight limp, as if one foot was heavier than the other. Voices muttered briefly and then Breece came back in and sat down at the table again.

I heard Finlay move into the front room.

"What's he doing?" I asked.

"Where's your dad, Martyn?"

"I don't know."

"What about your mom?"

"She doesn't live here."

"Where does she live?"

"I don't know."

He shook his head. "When did you last see your dad?"

I spooned tea bags from the cups, threw them at the waste-basket, and missed. "Saturday."

"Where?"

"Here. He went out."

"Where was he going?"

I poured milk into the teas, stirred them, and passed one to Breece. "To the pub, probably."

"And you haven't seen him since?"

I sat down at the table. "No."

"Aren't you worried?"

"He often stays away for days. He drinks."

Finlay came back in and stood by the window. He looked bored.

I didn't understand what was going on. What did they know? Did they know about Dad, or not? Why were they asking about Dean? I couldn't work out what to say, whether to lie or just say nothing. It's hard to lie convincingly when you don't know how much the other person knows.

Breece drained his cup, reached into his jacket pocket and pulled out some papers. He unfolded them and laid them out on the table for me to read.

Dear Mr. Pig, Further to our meeting on December first, I write to confirm that, as requested, a check in the amount of $60,000 was paid into your account this morning, being full payment. . . .

I looked up and met Breece's gaze. Pale blue eyes drilled into mine, unblinking. Wordlessly, he placed another sheet of paper on the table.

Signatures. *W. Pig. W. Pig. W. Pig. W. Pig* . . . Big droopy *W*, scrunched up little *PIG*.

I heard Alex's voice in my head — *You don't want to leave this lying around, do you? I'll flush it.*

"Letters addressed to William Pig," Breece said simply. "Your father."

"I don't know anything —"

"And forged signatures. These were found at Dean West's apartment this morning."

"Dean's?"

"He was killed in a road accident yesterday afternoon."

"Killed?"

"His motorcycle went under a bus. Just down the road, at the roundabout at the bottom of the hill. The brake lines failed."

"What?"

"Failed. Snapped. Possibly severed. Intentionally."

"I don't understand."

Breece stared at me for a moment, then reached into his pocket again and removed a clear plastic envelope, which he placed on the table. Inside it was a folded blue cloth. Like a washcloth. It *was* a washcloth. Mine.

"Sergeant Finlay just found this in your bathroom," said Breece.

There was a black smear smudged on the cloth.

Oil.

Brake line.

Dean.

Alex.

No, I thought. It's not real. Severed brake line? Not in real life. That's the kind of thing that only happens in books. It's ridiculous.

"I —" I began.

"Where's the oil from, Martyn?"

"I don't know."

"What was Dean West doing here?"

"He wasn't —"

"Where's your father?"

"I don't *know.*"

"Where were you yesterday afternoon at twelve-thirty?"

"I was here!"

"Sir," Finlay interrupted.

Breece looked up, annoyed. Finlay just looked at him. Some

kind of warning. Breece sighed and turned back to me, his voice calm. "Is there anyone you can call? A relative. An aunt, uncle?"

"What for?"

"We need to ask you some more questions. You're a minor. There has to be an adult present."

"I don't have any relatives."

"Friends? Neighbors?"

I shook my head.

Breece stood up. "Get your coat, Martyn."

"What for?"

He ignored me and turned to Finlay, buttoning up his raincoat. "Call Social Services, Don."

I don't know what kind of car it was, but it was a nice big one, warm and comfortable and quiet, with a dashboard full of softly lit dials. Finlay drove while Breece sat in the back with me. Up close, I could smell his sweat and the sour tang of whisky on his breath. We drove down Glory High Street, the car purring almost silently through the night. The snow had turned to a black winter rain. A single wiper scythed effortlessly across the rain-swept windshield, slicing back and forth like a thin black sword. *Shoosh-shush, shoosh-shush, shoosh-shush. . . .*

Although it was late the streets were still busy. Pockets of revellers swayed drunkenly along the pavements, shouting and laughing in the rain, their faces shining with alcohol. Some of them wore tinsel in their hair and Santa hats, others sprayed Silly String or blew tunelessly on party horns. Office parties, nightclubs, Christmas celebrations.

Finlay swore quietly as he swerved to avoid a drunk-eyed girl in a short sparkly dress tottering on high heels in the gutter.

Breece didn't seem to notice; he just sat there rigidly with his arms crossed, staring out at the rain. Fed up, probably. Working late. Christmas Eve.

I glanced at the clock on the dashboard — one o'clock in the morning.

It was Christmas Day.

The police station was clean and brightly lit. A low, pale brick building at the edge of town, it was surrounded by sparse lawns and smooth sloping driveways. A calming place. It was quiet. An oasis in a desert of small-town noise.

Inside, dark blue carpets covered the floors, deadening the sound of our footsteps as Breece led me past reception, through security doors, up a spiral staircase, and then along a series of long narrow corridors. Keyboards clacked softly behind half-open office doors. Muted telephones rang. The hiss of radio static crackled intermittently from unseen radios.

I was taken to a little room, like an office, at the end of a corridor. Breece sat me in a chair and told me to wait, then he left. A uniformed policewoman stood by the door with her hands behind her back, staring at the far wall. She was short and dumpy with a bob of mousy brown hair. A stern woman. I looked up at her and smiled but she didn't smile back.

It was a poky little place, no more than a cubicle, really. A desk, filing cabinets, two hard chairs against the wall, a water dispenser, bits of paper pinned to a wallboard. The desk was a cheap-looking thing made of fake black wood and cluttered with all kinds of stuff. Computer screen, keyboard, mugs full of pens, a telephone, a framed photograph of two young kids with a dog, unwashed coffee cups, empty sandwich wrappers, files, folders, sheets of paper scattered all over the place. I wondered how anyone could work like that. It was a mess.

Lists of green numbers glowed faintly from the computer screen. I studied them for a while but they didn't make any sense.

The policewoman cleared her throat and I turned to look at her, thinking she was about to say something, but she wasn't, she was just clearing her throat. She carried on staring at the wall. She was good at that.

Breece returned after about ten minutes, looking tired and irritated. Apparently, there was a problem getting hold of someone from Social Services. They were going to have to question me tomorrow.

"Does that mean I can go home?" I asked.

Breece smiled humorlessly and shook his head. "No."

I thought they were going to put me in a cell for the night, which would have been interesting. A cold, empty room with white walls and a concrete floor, a bunk bed, a lidless toilet, a peephole that slides up and down in the cell door. I could've sat on the edge of the bed holding my head in my hands, staring down at my feet, with moonlight from the barred window casting prison shadows across my face. But I was too young for that, it seems. So they put me in this odd little windowless room with a real bed, a carpet, a couple of chairs, a separate toilet and sink, pictures on the walls; there was even a little portable television. Very nice. It was like a cheap hotel room. Not that I've ever been in a cheap hotel room, but that's what I imagine one would be like.

The policewoman showed me into the room and stood by the door while I looked around.

"Make yourself at home," she said coldly.

I sat on the edge of the bed and took off my shoes.

"Thank you," I said.

She closed the door.

I should have known. I would have known. If it was a story, a murder mystery, I would have spotted the clues, I would have worked out what was happening. It was obvious.

Alex had killed Dean.

The footprints in the snow, leading across the street to Dean's motorcycle — they were hers. On Monday. She must have hurried back from Dean's apartment while he was at my house, cut the brake lines on his motorcycle, then sneaked across the road, walked down to the turn at the bottom of the hill, and waited for him. Hiding behind a parked car or something. Waiting for the sound of his brakeless motorcycle to come hurtling down the road. Watching, making sure. Witnessing his death. That's why she'd acted so strangely when she came back, rubbing her hands, listening to the ambulance siren. She'd just seen him die.

I should have known. I'd *heard* it. I'd heard Dean's motorcycle crash. Well, I hadn't actually heard it crash. But I'd heard it stop suddenly. At the bottom of the hill, at the turn. I'd heard it and I hadn't thought anything of it. *Acoustic illusion.*

Idiot.

The black smear on Alex's fingers, it was oil. I saw it. She must have wiped it off on the washcloth when she went upstairs to the bathroom. And that's probably when she'd taken the checkbook and everything, too. Pretending to be sick so I'd stay downstairs, same as when she took Dad's clothes.

That's OK. You can shut the door, lock it if you want. I'll be in the front room. Don't worry, I won't hear anything.

It was embarrassing.

But cutting the brake lines? That was unbelievable. Like something out of a comic strip. How did she know what to do? Where to cut? How to cut? What to cut? Unbelievable. She was an assassin. Alex the Assassin, cold-eyed and calculating, a hunter, a killer. . . .

That was it, I think. That was when the reality suddenly hit me. "Hey," it said, "this isn't one of your stupid childhood games. This isn't make-believe. It's *not* a murder mystery or something out of a comic strip. This is real. Think about it. She killed someone in cold blood. Your precious Alex actually *murdered* someone. . . ."

And as the truth sank in I felt my blood draining away.

Alex had killed Dean. Killed him. It wasn't an accident. It wasn't unintentional. It wasn't just one of those things. It was a premeditated act of revenge. He'd humiliated her, he'd made her feel like nothing. He'd used her. And he had to pay. I could understand that. I'd felt the same way myself. But *killing* him . . . ?

No.

It was too much. Too real. It was *real* real. Not just . . . well, not just whatever other *real* I'd been living in for the last week. It was *outside* real.

And it was too much to take.

As I sat there thinking about it my hands started shaking and then my stomach heaved and the next thing I knew I was kneeling in front of the toilet being sicker than I'd ever thought possible.

• • •

I've thought about it since, and I still don't quite understand it. I mean, I never liked Dean. I hated him. He was nothing, a stupid, worthless slob. He meant nothing to me. If he'd fallen off a cliff or died of a disease or something I wouldn't have shed any tears, so why did I feel so bad about Alex killing him? Why did it frighten me? What made it so *wrong*? The pain? The violence? The intention? The guilt? Did I feel sorry for him? Did I feel sorry for his parents, his brothers, his sisters. . . ?

I really don't know.

But something gripped me that night, and whatever it was it turned me inside out.

After I'd cleaned myself up and walked around the room for a while, my stomach began to settle and my hands eventually stopped shaking. I still didn't feel too good, though. My legs were hot and tingly, I was covered in sweat, and my head was throbbing. I couldn't think clearly. Disturbing images kept flashing through my mind: Dean's motorcycle crashing into the side of a bus; the sickening crunch of metal on metal; Alex rubbing her hands together, over and over again, rubbing, rubbing, rubbing. . . .

I sat down on the bed and stared at the floor, breathing steadily and keeping perfectly still. I don't know if it did any good, but I kept doing it, anyway, and after about ten minutes the headache eased and the images faded into the background. I was still sweating, but I could cope with that, and the hot tingling in my legs had cooled to a barely noticeable itch.

I was ready to start thinking again.

How did it happen?

Why did it happen?

Who thought of it?

Was the whole thing Alex's idea?

Did her mom put her up to it?

Or was it a bit of both?

I don't know. I suppose it all just fell into place. Luck. Fate. Destiny. Everything is determined. . . .

But however it happened, and whoever's idea it was, they'd certainly made the most of it. They'd thought of everything. They had the money, the tapes were gone, there was nothing to connect them with Dean, nothing to connect them with me, and nothing to connect them with Dad. And there was nothing I could do about it. Nothing Dean could do about it. Nothing Dad could do about it.

It was perfect.

The only thing I didn't understand was why Alex had left the lawyer's letters and forged signatures in Dean's apartment. They implicated Dean in Dad's death, that was obvious. But the police didn't know that Dad was dead. And even if they did, Dean was dead, too. So why make the connection? All it did was send the police to me. So, was Alex pointing the finger at Dean, or at me? Or both of us?

Or maybe she was . . .

It didn't really matter. None of it mattered. How, when, where, who, what, why . . . it didn't make any difference. It was done. All that mattered now was saving my own neck.

I stretched out on the bed and closed my eyes.

It was time for some serious thinking.

CHRISTMAS DAY

I was sitting on the edge of the bed tying my shoelaces when the door opened and Breece came in. It was eight o'clock in the morning. I hadn't slept. I'd spent most of the night sitting in a plastic chair, staring at the wall, and racking my brains. It wasn't easy. There was a lot to think about. There was also a lot to not think about, and not thinking about things is hard work, especially when your world has been turned upside down and you haven't slept for twenty-four hours. So, by the time Breece showed up I wasn't feeling too great, but I was as ready as I'd ever be.

Or so I thought.

Breece was wearing the same suit he'd been wearing the night before. Either he hadn't slept, or he only had one suit. From the bags under his eyes and the way he shuffled wearily into the room I guessed he hadn't slept. The policewoman who followed him in and closed the door looked friendlier than the one from the night before. Younger, prettier, with pale blond hair and a kind face.

"Morning, Martyn," said Breece. "This is Officer Sanders. Sally."

I nodded. Breece came over to the bed and sat down heavily beside me. He still smelled of sweat and tired whisky. "We've found your father," he said, looking me in the eye. "He's dead. I'm sorry."

When you're not sure what to do, it's always best to do nothing. So I did nothing, just stared at Breece with blank eyes. I hadn't expected this. I hadn't planned for this at all. How did they find him so fast? What should I do? *Do what you'd do if you were innocent*, the voice in my head told me. *Imagine it. You are innocent. You don't know anything about it.*

"Dead?" I said, stunned.

Breece was studying me. I could tell. The sympathetic look on his face couldn't hide the doubt in his eyes. I held his gaze. You don't *know* anything, I told him silently. You don't know anything. You might *think* you know, but you don't *know*. You can never know what's in my head. Only I know that. I know it. You don't know anything.

"I'm sorry," he said.

But there was no sorrow in his eyes, just a world-weary suspicion. He stood up and made way for Officer Sanders. Sally. As she sat down and put her arm around my shoulder I couldn't help noticing the sweet smell of her perfume — so sweet it was almost sickly. But not unpleasant. It reminded me of the scent that the girls in the fifth grade at school wear — cheap candy and flowers.

She put her hand on my knee and spoke quietly. "All right, Martyn?"

I nodded and started sniveling, watching Breece from the corner of my eye. Cold, hard eyes stared back at me from across the room. He didn't want to talk to me, he didn't want to be close, he just wanted to watch from a distance. Was I a sad young boy or a cold-hearted liar?

"How . . . how did he die?" I asked, beginning to sob.

"We don't know yet," Sally answered.

I stared at her hand on my knee. Small, slender, ringless fingers. Soft and clean.

I wiped snot from my nose. "When did it . . . when did it happen? Wh . . . where was he?"

Sally passed me a tissue and looked to Breece for advice. He nodded silently — tell him.

"His body was found at the quarry," she said.

"Where?"

"The old quarry. Do you know it?"

I shook my head and wiped at my eyes. "What happened? Was he drunk? Was it an accident?"

Sally looked to Breece again. He removed his hands from his pocket and ran a hand through his hair. "It's too early to tell," he said. "We'll talk about it later, when you feel up to it. We'll need to ask you some questions."

"What about?"

"Later." He tugged at the loose skin on his neck. "Your aunt is here."

Damn. How did they find her?

"She'd like to see you."

"No."

Breece eyed me suspiciously. "She's here now."

"I don't want to see her."

"Why not?"

"I just don't." I cried harder. Sally's hand tightened on my knee. "I don't have to, do I?"

"Well, no," said Breece. "Not if you don't want to. But I don't see —"

"I don't. I don't *want* to see her."

His eyes narrowed. He didn't like it, but there wasn't much he could do, was there? He couldn't *make* me see her. He rubbed at the stubble on his chin. "Do you want anything to eat? Some breakfast?"

I shook my head.

"Sally will stay with you for a while."

I sniffed and swallowed and tried to be brave. "No, thanks. I'm all right. I think I'd like to be on my own for a bit."

He shrugged and turned to go.

Sally gave me a final squeeze and a sad smile. "Are you sure, Martyn?"

"Yes," I mumbled.

She rose to follow Breece through the door.

"Inspector?" I said, just as the door was closing.

Breece stopped.

"Could I have a cup of tea, please?"

He stared at me for a second, nodded, then closed the door.

Not bad, I thought. Not bad at all. Pretty convincing. It's actually quite easy to make yourself cry. Alex told me how to do it.

All you do is think of something really sad. I thought about this dog I used to have when I was a kid. Jacko. A little brown mutt with a black eye patch. He was just a puppy. I really liked him. Loved him, I suppose. I'd never had a pet before. We used to go everywhere together. Me and Jacko. We were inseparable. Then, one day, I came home from school and he was gone. Dad had got rid of him because he kept peeing on the carpet. Sold him to someone down at the pub.

I don't think I ever got over that. Even thinking about it now there's tears in my eyes. He was a bastard, my dad, he really was.

After Breece left I thought about Jacko some more and carried on snuffling and looking distraught for a while. There were probably video cameras somewhere, behind the mirror, hidden in the wall. Breece might be sitting in the room next door, watching me on a blurred monitor. I wasn't falling for that.

A little later, Sally brought me a cup of tea. She reminded me of someone, but I couldn't think who it was. Someone on television. Her mouth . . . something about the shape of her mouth, that funny little pout . . . Polly, that's who it was. Polly whatever-her-name-is from *NYPD Blue*, the nice blond one. Polly the Policewoman.

"Cup of tea, Martyn," she said softly, placing the mug on the table with another sad smile.

"Thanks," I said mournfully.

After she'd gone I put my head in my hands and began crying again. This time the tears really poured out. Maybe I'd taken things too far, overdone it, made myself grieve so convincingly that even *I* was fooled. Or maybe it was just everything — Mom, Dad, Jacko, Alex, Dean, Aunty Jean, life, death, emptiness, whatever . . . everything. Maybe I'd just had enough of it all. Maybe. Who knows? Whatever the reason, I couldn't stop myself. I sat there on the edge of the bed and blubbered like a baby.

After a while the tears dried up and the sobbing eventually stopped. I felt drained. Tired. Dried up and sticky-eyed. I washed my face in cold water, drank some cold tea, then lay back on the bed.

It's hard work, crying. My body was absolutely exhausted. Dehydrated, I suppose. But my mind was clear again. I felt rejuvenated. I was back in control. The tears had sluiced away all the junk in my head. My mind was washed clean. Cleansed. Unjumbled. I could think.

I thought.

I didn't know how they'd found Dad, but they had. Which meant they would have found Dean's hair under his fingernails, found the cigarette butt, probably matched it with cigarette butts from his apartment. He'd be their prime suspect. Now Dean was dead and he was linked with me. Oil. Oil from Dean's motorcycle on a washcloth in *my* bathroom. First problem.

Second problem. They'd know I'd lied about Dean. Why? Why should I lie?

Third problem. I had to assume they'd searched the house. Was there anything in the house? Any evidence? Traces of the burned tapes? It wouldn't matter, they wouldn't know what they were. What about the tape we made of Dad snoring? Where was that? Did Alex take it? Did it matter? No. They wouldn't bother checking tapes unless they had a reason. Or would they?

No, surely not. Anything else? Dad's bedroom? The fireplace? Traces of blood? I cleaned it. What about the gloves? Shoes, clothes, fibers? Too much to think about.

Fourth problem. Letters, forged signatures in Dean's apartment. How? Why?

Fifth problem, sixth problem. . . .

I didn't understand how it had all gotten so complicated. It's never so complicated in books. Well, it is, but in a different way. Complications in stories are simple complications. Clues, plots, twists, and turns. Complicated but solvable. But these complications, real complications, these were all blurred together, all mixed up. It's like the difference between a well-constructed ball of string and a raggedy old pile of knots. With the ball of string you can get hold of one end, slowly unravel it and eventually you'll find out where it comes from. But with the pile of knots you pull on one end and the whole damn thing moves at once. All together. It's just a mess. The austere simplicity of fiction versus the tangled wool of fact. Who said that? Einstein again? No. Who was it? I don't know. I must have read it somewhere. Or did I? Maybe no one said it? Maybe I made it up myself?

Anyway, it was ridiculous. Everything was all knotted up together. Even I didn't know what was going on, and I was the one who'd started it all. I was lost in a raggedy old pile of knots.

My stomach rumbled. This time it wasn't nausea, it was hunger. I couldn't remember the last time I'd eaten anything and my stomach was empty from all that throwing up. I was starving. It was Christmas Day. I should be digging into a big plate of Christmas dinner. Turkey, potatoes, sausages, bacon, gravy, peas, carrots . . .

Forget it. You're in mourning, remember, you're too sad to eat.
I turned my attention back to the knots.

The interview room wasn't anything like the one in my dream. No bare concrete walls gleaming with condensation. No naked lightbulb. No hook-nosed Sherlock Holmes staring down at me with cruel eyes. It was just a room, an ordinary-looking office room: freshly painted walls, fluorescent light, a nice clean table, comfortable chairs; there was even a window. I could see pale clouds washing against a paper-white sky. The snow had stopped and the sun was out, just in time for Christmas.

The only similarities to my dream were the big black twincassette tape recorder set on a shelf against the wall, and me, sitting at the table, my hands sweating.

Sergeant Finlay reached across, inserted two cassettes in the tape recorder, and pressed a button. A high-pitched whine sounded briefly and a red light blinked. Across the table Inspector Breece looked bored as he loosened his tie.

"Interview with Martyn Pig commenced" — he glanced at his watch — "12.32 PM, December 25. Those present: Detective Inspector Samuel Breece, Detective Sergeant Donald Finlay, and —" He looked across at the man sitting next to me, inviting him to give his name.

"Peter Bennett," the man said.

"— and Peter Bennett from Social Services."

He was a weedy-looking young man with short ginger hair and a short ginger mustache that was hardly worth the bother of growing. It looked like a short ginger caterpillar. When Breece had introduced me to him half an hour earlier my first thought was that he looked like a bell ringer. His skin was sickly and colorless and his lips were too thin. He looked as if he didn't eat properly. He'd sat me down and explained the situation — you're not under arrest, you're free to leave whenever you like, you don't have to answer any of the questions, blah blah blah — but his voice was too boring to listen to and I found myself staring at his clothes. Brown suit jacket over a collarless white shirt, buttoned to the neck, new blue jeans, and brown slip-on shoes. He can't make up his mind what he wants to be, I thought. Smart businesslike professional or cool young dude? I could have told him it didn't matter, whatever he wore he'd look like a bell ringer.

Now, I watched as he snapped open a slim brown briefcase, removed a notepad and pen, then replaced the briefcase on the floor beneath the table. Breece watched him, too, with barely disguised disdain, waiting while he opened the notepad, found a fresh page, clicked his pen, then looked up with eager eyes.

"Ready?" asked Breece with a hint of sarcasm.

"Go ahead, Inspector," Bennett replied, pen poised.

Breece turned his haggard attention to me. "You understand that you're here of your own free will, Martyn?"

I didn't think I was, but I nodded anyway.

"Could you answer out loud, please, for the benefit of the tape."

"Yes," I said.

"You don't have to answer any questions if you don't want to; you're not under arrest. We just want to clear up a few things."

"Right."

"Good." Breece glanced down at his own notepad. "When we spoke to you at your home on Tuesday night, you said you'd last seen your father on Saturday."

"Yes."

"Are you sure?"

"Sure that I said it or sure that it was Saturday?"

He looked at me. "I'll ask you again. When did you last see your father?"

"Saturday. That's when he started feeling better."

"Better? What do you mean?"

"He was ill."

"When?"

"When what?"

"When was he ill?"

I looked up at the ceiling thoughtfully. "At least until Friday. That's when Aunty Jean came over. She'll tell you. She saw him. He was still in bed then. Flu or something."

"But he was better on Saturday?"

"Yes. He started feeling better in the morning, then later on, about five or six, he told me he was going out."

"Did he say where?"

I shook my head. "Just out."

"What did you do when he didn't return?"

"Nothing. I told you, he often didn't come back. He drank a lot."

Breece stared at me for a moment, disbelief evident in his eyes. I looked down at the table and glanced across at Bennett's notepad. The page was filled with neat, girly writing — big, round letters in pale blue ink. Circles for dots. His pen, an expensive-looking gold thing, hovered over the page, waiting for the interview to go on.

Breece rose from the table, hitched up his pants and walked to the window. "Do you own a sleeping bag, Martyn?"

I looked bemused. "A sleeping bag?"

"A sleeping bag."

I glanced at Bennett.

"Is this relevant, Inspector?" Bennett asked.

Breece ignored him. "Do you own a sleeping bag?" he repeated.

"No," I replied.

"Are you sure?"

"Why should I?"

"I fail to see the rele —" Bennett began.

"Mr. Bennett, the question is relevant to our inquiry. Please allow Martyn to answer."

Bennett scribbled petulantly in his notepad, and Breece went on. "What about your father? Did he own a sleeping bag?"

"I don't know," I said. "He might have. I don't know."

Breece glanced over my shoulder at Finlay, blinked, then looked back at me. "Your father's body was found inside a sleeping bag. Fibers similar to those found in the sleeping bag were removed from your house last night by forensics officers."

"Inside a sleeping bag?" I said, bewildered.

"Inspector . . ." Bennett piped up in his for-goodness-sake-this-is-a-child-you're-talking-to voice.

Breece ignored him again. He walked slowly back to the table and sat down, watching me all the time with an expression that managed to convey both concern and distrust. "The sleeping bag was stapled together, weighed down with stones, and then sunk in a water-filled gravel pit."

"Really, Inspector!" Bennett snapped as he jumped up out of his chair. "I can't allow this!"

Breece raised his head slowly and fixed Bennett with an insolent glare. "Sit *down*, Mr. Bennett."

"You're going too far, Inspector. Martyn's —"

"Sit down, Mr. Bennett," Breece ordered.

Bennett's face glowed red as he lowered himself back into his chair. I almost felt sorry for him.

Breece went on. "Preliminary reports indicate that your father may have been dead for some time."

"I don't understand," I said.

"Neither do we. That's why we're talking to you." He paused, scratching absently at the back of his neck. "Is there anything you want to tell me, Martyn? Anything you might have *forgotten*?"

"About what?"

"Anything." He paused. "Dean West, for example."

This was the tricky part. I hesitated. "Maybe . . ."

Breece leaned back in his chair. "Maybe?"

I waited, blinking my eyes, looking nervous. "I was scared."

"Scared of what?"

"Of him, Dean."

"Why were you scared of him?"

"He said he was going to get me."

"When?"

"A couple of weeks ago," I explained, stuttering, trying not to cry. "There was a Christmas dance, an end-of-term thing at school. I was talking to a girl. That's all I was doing, just talking to her. I didn't know she was Dean's girlfriend."

From behind me, Finlay spoke for the first time. "What's her name?"

I didn't turn around. "I don't know. I only spoke to her for a minute or two. She was on her own, waiting in the corridor. We just started talking. She seemed quite friendly. She was pretty. We were just talking. Then Dean appeared at the end of the corridor and she suddenly got frightened and told me I'd better go. He was her boyfriend, she said; he didn't like her talking to other boys. I thought she was just being stupid, you know, trying to impress me. But she looked really scared. So I decided to go. Just as I turned to leave I heard Dean shout out something and then he started to come after me."

"What did you do?"

I shrugged. "I ran. He looked angry, mad. I think he was drunk."

"Then what?"

"I just ran. I don't know if he followed me, I didn't look back. I went home. I didn't think any more about it. But then, a couple of days later, I started hearing rumors that he was after me, that he knew who I was and that he was going to get me."

Breece looked puzzled. "Because of the girl?"

"I suppose so."

"And you don't know her name?"

"No."

"How old was she?" Finlay asked. "What did she look like?"

"About sixteen, seventeen. My height, short blond hair, pretty."

"Was she someone from school?"

"No. I'd never seen her before."

"What was Dean doing at a school dance?" Breece asked.

"I don't know. He was there with some other bikers."

Breece frowned. He wasn't happy. "You have seen him recently, then?"

I nodded, then remembered the tape and said, "Yes."

"When?"

"Last week," I said remorsefully. "He came by my house."

"When?"

"Thursday. With one of his biker friends."

"Name?" said Finlay.

"I don't know. He was shorter than Dean, slighter, younger, with straggly black hair. They came into the house . . . I thought they were going to get me. . . ." I shuddered at the memory.

Breece shot another glance at Finlay. "Go on."

"Dad couldn't help me, he was ill, fast asleep, upstairs in bed. Dean pushed me around a bit, told me to stay away from his girlfriend or he'd kill me."

"He said that? That he'd kill you?"

"Yes. Then he asked me if there was any money in the house. He said if I didn't give him some money him and his friend would hurt me. I told him there wasn't any, we didn't have any money, but he didn't believe me. Then he started searching everywhere, pulling out drawers, looking in pots, all over the place, but he couldn't find anything. I was really scared, he was acting crazy. He told his friend to watch me while he went upstairs. I heard him searching through my bedroom, then Dad's room. . . ."

"He went into your father's room?"

"Yes. He was everywhere. When he came back down he was carrying some letters and he had this crazy grin on his face.

They were the letters you showed me, the ones about Dad's money, the will. I didn't know anything about it."

Bennett spoke up. "Just a minute, Martyn. You don't have to —"

"It's all right," I said, "I want to tell them what happened."

"Yes, I know, but —"

"I *want* to. All right?"

Bennett pouted and went back to his notepad.

I went on. "Dean showed me the letters and told me he wanted the money, all of it. Sixty thousand dollars. I told him I didn't know anything about it, it was Dad's money. It was probably in the bank. But he didn't care. He was all wound up, like he was on drugs or something. He told me he'd be back on Monday and if I didn't have the money then, he'd kill me."

"Why didn't you report this to us?" asked Breece.

"He told me that if anything happened to him his friends would get me."

"Did he come back? On Monday?"

"Yes," I sniffed. "It was about lunchtime. I didn't know what to do. I was going to talk to Dad about it, but he was ill until Saturday, then he disappeared. I was on my own. I was scared, I didn't know what to do. I told Dean I couldn't get the money, I tried to explain, but he wouldn't listen, he was furious, ranting and raving, saying I was dead meat, I was history. . . ."

"Was he alone?"

"I don't know. I thought I saw someone on the back of his motorcycle when he arrived, the same one who was with him on Thursday, but Dean was alone when he came into the house, so I'm not sure. It was snowing, I couldn't see very well."

"What happened then?"

"He threatened me some more and . . . I don't know . . . he went upstairs for a bit, used the bathroom, then I heard him stomping around in Dad's room again. He had a bag with him, like a backpack. I think he was stealing stuff."

"What stuff?"

"I don't know. I never went in Dad's room. I don't know what he had."

"He definitely went into the bathroom?"

"Yes. I heard him."

"Then what?"

"Nothing really. When he came downstairs he said I had one more chance to get the money. He'd be back that night, with his friends this time." I shrugged. "But he never showed up."

The room was silent for a while. Bennett stopped writing and Breece just stared across the table at me, tugging at the skin of his neck, thinking. Behind me, I could hear Finlay scribbling in a notebook, and across the room the tape recorder whirred on, mindlessly recording the silence.

"Why didn't you tell me this earlier?" Breece asked.

I looked down, ashamed. "I was scared. I didn't know what to do. I'm sorry."

"Did you go anywhere near Dean's motorcycle, at any time?"

"No."

"Did you see anyone else go near it?"

"No. Unless there *was* someone on the back of it when he arrived, you know, the one who was with him on Thursday."

"Did you see Dean with a sleeping bag?"

"No."

"What about in his bag? You said he had a backpack. Could there have been a sleeping bag in his backpack? Or anything else?"

I thought about that. "Maybe," I said, "I don't know."

"About this money —"

"I think that's enough for now, Inspector," Bennett interrupted.

"I have a few more ques —"

"I *am* a bit tired, actually," I said. Which was putting it mildly. Lying's a tiring business, and together with no sleep and nothing to eat, I was just about ready to drop.

Breece studied me again. It was hard to tell what he was thinking now. But at least I'd given him something to think about.

"All right," he said eventually, looking at his watch. "Interview terminated at 13:02 PM." He nodded at Finlay to turn off the tape recorder.

"Can I go home, now?" I asked.

Breece stood up and stretched, glancing at Bennett.

Bennett said, "We can't let you stay in the house on your own, Martyn."

"Why not?"

"You're too young."

"I've done it before."

"I dare say you have," he said, neatly packing his notepad and pen back into his briefcase. "Your aunt has kindly offered to look after you."

"No way," I said.

"Pardon?"

"I'm not going with her."

"Why not?"

"I'm not. I'm not going to."

Bennett's thin lips smiled. "I'm afraid there's nowhere else."

"I'll stay here."

Finlay found that amusing and grinned quietly to himself.

"You can't stay here," Bennett said.

His stupid voice, the way he talked to me like I was mental or something, I felt like punching him in the mouth. I knew I would if this carried on much longer. So I shut up.

Bennett took my silence for acceptance. "I'll give you a lift to your aunt's. We can talk on the way, sort things out."

I'll sort you out, I thought.

Breece was watching me from across the room. I knew he didn't believe me. He knew I was lying. And I knew he didn't know why. But what could he do?

"Is that all, Inspector?" Bennett asked.

Breece didn't take his eyes off me.

"Inspector?"

Breece turned to Bennett and looked at him like he was a bad smell. Bennett pursed his lips. There was an awkward silence, then Breece shrugged, nodded, and began to clear his stuff from the desk. "We'll need to speak to you again," he said to me.

"I won't leave town," I replied.

He grinned coldly but said nothing. Finlay was writing something on the back of the tapes. He pocketed them, closed his notebook, glanced at Breece, then went to wait by the door. Breece put his jacket on and started across the room.

"How did you find him?" I asked.

Breece froze. "What?"

"My dad. How did you find him?"

"Divers."

"Yes, but how did you know he was there?"

"Know he was where?"

"In the gravel pit. You told me, he was sunk at the bottom of a gravel pit, weighed down with rocks."

"Stones, I said."

"Stones, rocks, what's the difference?"

The hint of a smile flickered on his craggy old face. He clipped his pen into his jacket pocket. "Anonymous phone call," he explained. "Three o'clock this morning from a stolen mobile phone. Gave us the precise location of the body. Male voice, fortyish maybe, sounded drunk." He buttoned his jacket. "Any ideas?"

"No," I said, a shade too quickly.

Breece raised an eyebrow and opened the door.

"Is that it?" I asked.

"For now."

It was bright outside. Cold, bright, and humdrum. Another reality. It was like coming out of the cinema into the late afternoon daylight when everything feels dull and pale and flat. The light, the smell of the air, the sound of the sparse Christmas Day traffic — all too real. Peter Bennett marched along beside me through the station parking lot, swinging his car keys in one hand and his stupid briefcase in the other, prattling away about God-knows-what. But I wasn't listening. I was thinking of Alex.

Alex.

You thought of everything, didn't you?

And that's about it, really. That's just about all I'm going to tell you. I've been at Aunty Jean's for almost a year now. It's not as bad as I thought it would be. Although that's not to say it's great or anything. There's plenty of Aunty's crap to deal with. She's forever trying to *educate* me, for one thing. Constantly introducing me to what she thinks are the social niceties of life — boring little parties, nice people, manners, hobbies. Social education, she calls it. "Get yourself a decent hobby, Martyn, for goodness sake — hiking, bird-watching, something healthy. You can't spend all day lying on your bed reading detective books."

Why not?

And she always wants to know where I'm going, where I've been, who I've been with. Not that it really matters; I hardly ever go anywhere. And even when I do I don't tell her anything. I just lie. But still, it gets on my nerves.

At least her house is quite nice. Semidetached, on the other side of town, nice and quiet with plenty of room. And she's all right for money, too. So things aren't too bad.

The funny thing is, it turns out she's a drinker, too. Just like Dad. It must run in the family. She makes out that she only drinks *socially* — sherry, cocktails, that kind of thing — but she's got bottles hidden all over the place. Under the sink, in the cupboards, in the bathroom. Gin, mostly. You wouldn't know

EPILOGUE

she's drunk a lot of the time, she covers it up pretty well, a lot better than Dad. But some nights, after she's been sipping all day, I see her stumbling up the stairs, red-faced and boozy, wall-eyed, mumbling drunkenly to herself. She pretends she has a head cold, holds a scented handkerchief to her mouth to hide the smell of the drink. But it's all right, I don't really mind. She doesn't get violent or anything, she's more of a maudlin drunk. She just cries a lot. Nice, quiet, drunken tears.

The whole Dad and Dean thing never came to anything. There was a coroner's inquest, of course, then a couple of weeks of madness with all the newspapers and the television people crawling all over the place. And then the funeral, which I hated. It was terrible. Sitting in this stupid chapel with a load of people I didn't know, all silent, their eyes carefully avoiding the cloth-covered box waiting patiently at the front while taped funeral music groaned out from hidden speakers. I remember looking around, staring at all these miserable faces, wondering who on earth they were. That old woman dressed in a sad sack of a black dress clutching a limp black handbag in her lap, the one with blank orbs for eyes. Who's she? Those two ferretlike men with gaunt faces sitting rigidly beneath the high window. Who are they? And that tarty blond woman snuffling noisily into a tiny white handkerchief, tugging at the hem of her short black skirt as if she can't understand why it's so short. Do I know you?

Breece was there, sitting unobtrusively at the back, dressed in the same blue suit he always wore. And there were one or two others I recognized: Aunty Jean, of course, a couple of fat drunks from Dad's pub, the man from the off-licence. But the rest of them were strangers. Strangers in a strange place.

After a good half hour or so of depressing music, the priest stood up and started spewing out a load of garbage about Dad. Good man, God's will, final resting place, blah blah blah . . . I tried not to listen, staring instead at the coffin perched on a gurney just a few feet in front of me. Dad in a plywood box, lying there as nothing in the hollow darkness. I wondered what he looked like now.

Hymns, prayers, more words, more hymns. Stand up, sit down, close your eyes, open your eyes, stand up, sit down . . . then, eventually, the words dried up, the gurney rolled, the curtains closed and the box was gone.

And that was that.

The case is still officially open, but I haven't seen Breece or Finlay for months now. Breece kept digging away at first, asking thousands of questions, interviewing people, searching for evidence, but he never got anywhere. The ball of string was too knotty. He found plenty of stuff, but it was all just bits and pieces, nothing that would fit together well enough to prove anything. He knew I had *something* to do with it, but he couldn't work out what. I think he was pretty sure that Dean killed Dad — the hairs and cigarette butt in the sleeping bag, the letters and signatures in his apartment, the story I made up about him — but, again, he couldn't prove it. And, what's more, he couldn't see a reason for it. Why would Dean want to kill Dad? If he was trying to get hold of Dad's money, why kill him?

As to who killed Dean, I think he had me pegged for that. But there was nothing he could do about it. My story — the school dance, the girlfriend, the mysterious black-haired biker friend — that got checked out pretty thoroughly. No one remembered seeing me talking to a pretty blond girl, no one even remembered seeing me at the dance. But then again, no one could prove I *wasn't* there, either.

One of my neighbors — the woman from number seven, the slip-flashing cancan dancer — she confirmed she'd seen a tall boy with a ponytail outside my house on the Thursday and again on the Monday. She *thought* there might have been some-one else with him, someone who *might* have been shorter than Dean, who *may* have had black hair. She *might* have seen some-one squatting down behind a parked motorcycle fiddling with the wheels, but she wasn't sure. It could even have been a girl.

Maybe, if, might have, could have been. . . .

As to what happened to the sixty thousand dollars, I don't think Breece had a clue. Video footage from security cameras at the bank showed a blurred figure cashing a check for sixty thousand dollars on the Tuesday morning. Despite being well wrapped up against the cold in a coat, scarf, and hat, the blurred figure still bore a passing resemblance to Mr. William Pig. Same size, same age, same grubby brown jacket beneath the coat, same shambling gait and baggy eyes. But how could that be? The autopsy had proved that Dad was already dead by then. And so was Dean. So who the hell was it?

Not me, that's for sure. I'm way too short.

Aunty Jean gave a sworn statement saying that Dad was still alive on Friday. He was ill in bed; she said, he'd looked like death warmed over.

There weren't any tire tracks or footprints at the gravel pit, the ground was too hard, frozen solid. Dean's fingerprints in my house proved he'd been there, but the only prints upstairs — apart from mine and Dad's and Aunty Jean's — couldn't be identified. So maybe there was someone with Dean when he came over on the Monday? Or maybe Dad had a mysterious lady friend? Who knows? (I always wondered if Breece had contacted Maeve, the not-*that*-lonely heart. It wasn't something I lost sleep over, exactly, but I sort of hoped he hadn't.) My fingerprints were all over the place, of course. But I lived there, so that proved nothing.

Someone remembered seeing some kind of car or van parked outside my house on Saturday evening, someone else thought they heard someone shouting. . . . The list was endless, dozens of scraps of puzzling evidence all of which proved absolutely nothing at all.

You see, it doesn't matter what the police *think*, it doesn't matter what they *know*, all that matters is proof. If they can't prove something, there's nothing they can do. Nothing. They're stumped. That's the way it is, that's the way it works. That's justice.

After about two or three months, the whole thing began to

fizzle out. The case was wound down, put on the back burner. It was a waste of time.

Alex was only ever mentioned once. Breece had dropped in on one of his frequent visits, questioning me again about something or other. I'd grown used to it. It's easy. All you've got to do is stick to what you've already said, and if anything tricky comes up, you can't remember. And when in doubt, say nothing. Anyway, it must have been somewhere around the end of April. We were in the conservatory at Aunty Jean's house. My house. Aunty Jean was spring-cleaning. I could see her through the French windows, polishing like a nutcase in the front room, stooped over the dining table with her sleeves rolled up, her polishing arm pumping away like a piston. Spring sunshine flooded in through the open conservatory doors; a smell of fresh flowers breezed in the air. Breece was slouched in a wicker chair, bored, sipping tea from a cup, looking wearier than ever. Same old worn-out suit, same old worn-out face. He was just rambling on about something when suddenly, without warning, he stopped in mid-sentence and said, "How well did you know Alexandra Freeman?"

I nearly choked on my tea. "Who?"

"Alexandra Freeman. She lived down the road from you."

"Oh, right. Alex. Yes. I remember her."

"Was she a friend?"

"No, not really. Well, sort of. We hung around together sometimes . . . you know."

"No, I don't know."

I shrugged.

"Did she ever come to your house?"

"Once or twice."

"Once or twice? No more than that?"

"Maybe a couple of times more. I can't remember, really." I swallowed. "Why do you ask?"

He put down his tea and looked out of the window. "Nice garden."

"Yes." I followed his gaze. It was a nice garden. A long stretch of well-tended lawn bounded by neat flower beds, shrubs, several young willow trees, and a small rockery dotted with frosty-green alpine plants. Nice and quiet. Peaceful.

"Do you mow it?"

"What?"

"The lawn," he said. "Do you mow it?"

"No."

He covered his mouth and coughed, a thick phlegmy rattle. "What did you and Alexandra do together?"

"Nothing much. Like I said, I didn't know her that well."

"You spoke on the phone quite frequently."

"Did we?"

"Very frequently, according to the telephone records."

I didn't know what to say.

"Especially around Christmastime," Breece went on. "Two, three times a day. Sometimes more."

"She was helping me with something."

He raised an eyebrow.

"A project," I said. "A school project."

"A project."

"Homework. For the Christmas holidays. About the theater. Alex knew a lot about acting, she went to drama classes. She was helping me with the project."

Breece nodded thoughtfully. "That was nice of her."

"Yes . . . she was like that. Very helpful."

"Have you seen her recently?"

"I think she moved away."

"When would that have been?"

"I don't know . . . soon after Christmas, I think."

"Any idea where?"

"No. Sorry."

He said nothing for a minute or two, gazing out at the garden, tugging occasionally at his earlobe. It was a beautiful day. Cloudless blue skies, willow trees waving gently in a slow breeze, birds singing. A lawn mower droned comfortably in the distance.

Breece leaned forward in his chair, looked me in the eye, and spoke softly.

"How does it feel, Martyn?"

"What?"

"Getting away with murder."

I paused for a second, then answered calmly. "I don't know what you mean."

He smiled. The first time I'd ever seen him smile. "No . . . I don't suppose you do."

• • •

That was almost the last time I saw him. I think maybe he came around once or twice afterward, but he never mentioned Alex again. By then he was just going through the motions. I could tell by the look in his eyes that he'd just about given up.

I got a letter from her yesterday. From Alex.

I don't usually bother with the mail, there's never anything for me, but I just happened to be passing the door when the mailman shoved a load of stuff through the box. Even then, I normally would have left it, but Aunty Jean called out from the kitchen, "Is that the mail? Bring it through, Martyn, that's a dear."

That's another thing I hate, she calls me *dear*.

It was an airmail letter in a light-blue envelope. The postmark was smudged: somewhere, something, California. Addressed to me. From Alex. Her handwriting. I held the envelope in my hand and stared at my name. *M. Pig*. Her handwriting. It burned a hole in my heart. I couldn't breathe. Then Aunty called out again — "Martyn! *Martyn!* What *are* you doing out there?" — and I came to my senses and sucked some air into my lungs. I shoved the letter into my pocket, delivered the rest of the mail to Aunty, then rushed upstairs to my room.

It was only one page. One thin page. The paper felt so fragile in my hand, as if it would melt away. As I read the words I could hear her voice in my head. It was unreal. Like in a film, where you see the hero, alone in his room, reading a love letter, and in the background you hear the disembodied voice of his lover. That's exactly what it felt like. Exactly.

• • •

Dear Martyn,

If you're reading this at your aunty's then it means everything turned out OK for you, so I hope you are. If not — well, I'm sorry. I tried to leave things pointing in the right direction.

You told me once that badness is a relative thing — you said that something's only wrong if you think it's wrong. That if you think it's right, and others think it's wrong, then it's only wrong if you get caught. I didn't understand what you meant at the time. But now, I think I do. I hope you still believe it. If not . . . well, what can I say?

Anyway, here I am in the USA and I've finally made it as an actress. I got my first role last week. It's only a commercial, but at least it's a start. It's for a deodorant. I have to walk up and down the beach in a bikini looking cool. What do you think of that? I'll be on television. I've got auditions lined up for good parts, too — films, theater, musicals. Real acting.

So you'd better hurry up and write that murder mystery you told me about, the one where I play the murderer's beautiful mistress, because if you leave it much longer I'll be too famous to star in it — you won't be able to afford me!

So get writing, Martyn.

I'm sure you can think up a story.

Love, A.

I put down the letter and looked out of the window.

It was starting to snow.

ABOUT THE AUTHOR

Kevin Brooks has led a varied career, including jobs at a railroad station, a crematorium, and the London Zoo. He is married and lives in Essex, U.K. (officially the smallest town in England). His greatest literary heroes are Jack Kerouac, Raymond Chandler, Cormac McCarthy, and, of course, J.D. Salinger. *Martyn Pig* is his first novel.